HALLOWED EVE

SUZA KATES

ICASM PRESS
SAVANNAH

Published by Icasm Publishing LLC

5710 Ogeechee Rd. Suite 200 #278, Savannah, GA 31405

www.icasmpress.com

Library of Congress Cataloging-in-Publication Data

Kates, Suza

Hallowed Eve / Suza Kates

p. cm.

ISBN-13:978-0-9845929-5-1
ISBN-13:978-0-9845929-7-5 (ebook)

I. Title

Printed and bound in the United States of America

10 9 8 7 6 5 4 3 2 1

For Information on

Current Releases
Upcoming Releases
Book Signings
Newsletter
Giveaways

Visit

www.suzakates.com

For Information on

Current Releases
Upcoming Releases
Book Signings
Newsletter
Giveaways

Visit

www.suzakates.com

One

Nowhere is safe.

With cool palms and thumping heart she stared down her current nemesis as it loomed over her, solid and seemingly impenetrable. It was just a door. Made of thick, antique oak that had long ago been dyed the color of good cooking sherry.

For Eve Taylor, it might as well have been the gateway to hell.

If any place in the world should offer security and familiarity, it was her grandmother's home. The old glass doorknob was dull but still as fascinating as when she'd been a little girl and believed the house filled with huge diamonds. It should have been a comfort, a dear reminder of a loved one, but she just couldn't force her trembling hand to grasp it and turn.

Eve mentally chastised herself. *It's too dark down there. What the hell am I thinking?* She couldn't believe she was actually considering going in and breaking the cardinal rule.

No basements. Especially if she was alone.

She only wanted to run down for her grandmother's stand mixer, knowing it would be easy to find, tucked neatly away in a box on a shelf, sealed with strong tape and marked clearly with Eve's name. That had been her grandmother's way.

She wanted, actually she needed, the mixer for reasons other than nostalgia. It would be a helpful addition for her soon-to-open business and would cut prep-time in half. However, the brilliant idea of giving it a test-run with chocolate cupcakes didn't hold the same thrill as it had moments before. The huge door waiting for her next move dampened the excitement. She'd been in the house a couple of days and had thus far kept it closed and dead-bolted, feeling more at ease with the dingy basement cloistered away from the rest of the house.

A glance at the cooking supplies she'd picked up renewed her fortitude. She would be quick about it. In and out like a flash. Decision made, Eve put her hand on the knob without looking, felt the glass under her clammy flesh, and turned it with a jerk, shoving the door open before her mind could change.

The emptiness of the cellar opened below her in silent invitation. She slapped her hand on the switch to illuminate the room and took one timid step at a time, trying to imagine the smell of freshly baked chocolate as encouragement.

Chilly air enveloped her in an unwelcome grasp, making her arm hairs stand on end. One lonely bulb hung by a wire, struggling to light the room, and she knew it was likely a mistake to venture down the old wooden stairs, each step creaking in protest.

Or in warning, depending on one's perspective.

Both tennis shoes finally found purchase on the floor, and Eve took a moment to inspect her surroundings. Not much had changed over the years. Her grandmother still kept Woolite on the shelf above the washer, but the machine itself was a modern, energy saving brand and boasted a shiny, sea-green exterior that matched the sleek dryer beside it.

Eve smiled at her grandmother's splash of color in the musty work space and was encouraged by the elderly woman's use of the subterranean room. If Nan could come down often enough to do laundry, Eve would find enough spine to last a few minutes.

Rolling her shoulders as if preparing for battle, she took a step toward the shelving unit, but her muscles froze, and the smile slipped from her face.

The evil had found her after all.

"It's not real. It's not real." She whispered the mantra to

herself again and again, clenching her fists to her stomach as she recited the words. Hoping the little girl wouldn't be there when she looked again, Eve forced her eyes shut until they ached and blue flashes exploded in the dark behind her lids. Pain crawled from one temple to the other, leaving an aching trail behind it in her head.

Deciding one more time for good measure, she spoke the magic even louder. "It's not real."

And opened her eyes.

The girl was still there, piled in the corner. Her small body flat and lifeless on the cold, rough cement. No place for the delicate skin of a child.

Eve had known coming home to Pine Creek would rustle up old memories. They lurked like demons, waiting for an opportunity and knowing just when to strike. It had been months since an attack had punched at her like this, but she should have expected as much.

No basements.

This was one hellcat of an image, and all of her senses were being assaulted. She blinked, but could still see the body. She could smell mold and dirt. Far away, she would swear there was the sound of crying.

Eve told herself again it was all in her head. She knew the gloominess and dank, earthy scent had triggered an episode. The images were nothing more than symptoms of her episodes, or attacks. That's what she called them, because she would never use the word vision. That made her sound psychic, and since she was definitely not cerebrally enhanced, the only option left was plain-stinking-nuts.

So, she called them attacks, something akin to mild anxiety. That was doable. She could live with a little panic now and then, but didn't care to be strapped down and shot up with Haldol.

Blowing out a frustrated breath, Eve closed her eyes again and tried to will the grisly sight into non-existence. *One more*

*time. The girl is not real, and she will not be there when I open
my eyes. Ready. One...two...three...open.*

She saw pale, thin arms and legs in a tangle. The long red
hair that had once been braided in two long plaits and held
in an upward curve by coat-hanger wire so they would look
like Pippi Longstocking. The girl wore a shapeless dress and
striped blue and white tights to complete the outfit.

But her blaze of hair was now disheveled and dirty. It was
knotted and matted, sticky with what looked like...

Rat-tat-tat-tat-tat! Rat-tat-tat!

Eve's skin shifted over her bones and cold tightened her
scalp. It took her a moment and three panicked breaths to
realize someone was knocking on the glass of the kitchen door
upstairs.

Placing her hand over her heart in an attempt to slow it
down, she threw a leery look toward the shadowed corner. The
surge of adrenaline from being startled must have made a
scrambled mess of her brain chemicals, because the image was
finally gone. Nothing but an empty corner with a few terra-
cotta planters.

Foolishness heated and blushed her face. It had been stupid
to break the rule. Angry with herself and still shaken, she
swore to find a way to regain control of her tainted mind.

As soon as she was out of here and away from this town.

The persistent knocking sounded once again.

An encouraging thought swayed her. Maybe it would be
Lance, and she could ask him to come down to retrieve the
mixer. Taking a tentative step backwards up the stairs, Eve
decided it sounded like the perfect solution.

She'd had enough therapy for one day.

Lance would have no trouble taking the burden for his little
sister. He would understand. He had been there when it all
happened.

~~~

On the other side of the window panes, a peacock-blue scarf fluttered in the autumn breeze. This alone was evidence of who stood outside.

"I thought you weren't coming until later," Eve said as she opened the door.

Gabrielle Del Maro shook flowing brown hair out of her face and met Eve's stare head-on. "You know how I feel about schedules." The woman's smile sparkled as much as her light brown eyes. She absolutely radiated life, and Eve always felt like a blue-eyed Amazon next to her.

"Gabrielle," Eve said with a mixture of relief and gratitude as she hugged her, then pulled back to see what hard object was between them.

"Here. I brought you some wine. A housewarming gift." Gabrielle shook the bottle in the air. "It's your favorite."

Eve cocked her head. "Cabernet? That's your favorite, but good try."

Her friend whipped another bottle from behind her back. "I remembered. Something sweet and light for the connoisseur, though how a chef doesn't fill her blood with the heady splash of rich red, I'll never understand."

Taking the offerings and heading to the ancient white Frigidaire with rust at the edges, Eve spoke over her shoulder. "I'm not technically a chef, you know."

"That's right. You're a genius. Wasting your talent by managing someone else's restaurant, to prepare yourself, and learn about the business side, and blah, blah, blah." Gabrielle pulled two glasses from a cabinet and settled herself on a stool at the large wooden table that served as an island.

Deciding it was her day to be daring, Eve pulled up a seat and motioned with her finger, indicating she'd try some of the darker wine Gabrielle was uncorking. "You'll be happy to know that my days of organizing and number crunching for someone else are over. For the most part, anyway. I've cut my hours down to less than part-time. Now," she emphasized, "that I have learned about the business side."

Gabrielle scrutinized her and nodded. "You can tell me all about it, but first take a nice, long drink. You're as pale as one of those creepy bald cats with all the wrinkles."

Grimacing at the comparison, Eve did as instructed then cringed again at the taste of tannic acid. She remembered why she stuck to the light stuff. "It shows, does it?"

"It does. Did something happen?" Gabrielle paused. "Oh, honey, are you upset about Nan?"

At the mention of her grandmother, Eve glanced away before speaking. "I am, of course, but that's not why...I, uh, well... I went into the basement."

"Holy Hannah."

"You said it," Eve whispered, slapping a hand to her forehead. "I know better, I do, but I just planned to run down and grab Nan's mixer. I've had control of things for a while, and I guess I got a little cocky."

"Her mixer?" Gabrielle jumped up and patted Eve's arm. "I know just where it is, because she told me to make sure you got it. Guess I'm a minute late."

For such a small woman, Gabrielle sounded like a buffalo tramping down the same steps Eve had so carefully traversed only moments before. Eve took another sip of wine, wishing she could charge so easily into darkness.

Soon her friend was back and setting a box on the floor. Sure enough, it was neatly taped and had Eve's name on it.

"Thanks, Gab. I don't suppose you'll want to stay for the cupcakes? Chocolate top and bottom." Eve felt the panic from earlier slipping out of her system. A little food, drink, and girl talk would put her right.

"Without a doubt. Besides, we don't get many opportunities to hang out." A shadow passed behind Gabrielle's eyes. "I sure do miss you, Eve."

Eve tilted her head and sighed as a familiar longing blossomed inside her chest. "I miss you, too, and everyone. But you know I can't stay. I've built a life somewhere else."

"You rent a tiny apartment you hardly ever see because you're working sixty hours a week for that task-master you call a boss."

"I told you, I'm done with that. I've been working from home and am planning to launch the business soon." Eve held up a hand at the protest she could see forming on Gabrielle's lips. "You can't change my mind about moving back. I'm only here now because of Nan's funeral and to settle her affairs."

Gabrielle shrugged in defeat. "So what's next?"

"Lance and I meet with the lawyer tomorrow. Mom and Dad are having us deal with it, since they couldn't get back in time." Eve lifted one side of her mouth in an amused grin. "They would have been here, but it took days to track them down. Survival camp in Colorado."

"What will they think of next in their quest to be the most adventurous retirees in Georgia?" Gabrielle asked. She had spent many of her teenage days at Eve's house and knew the Taylor family well. "Never mind. I'm almost afraid to know."

Slapping her hands on the table, Eve stood and knotted her hair up with a scrunchie. "Enough talk. Let's cook."

Gabrielle lifted her glass in a toast. "And drink."

Sauntering over to the radio, Eve twisted a knob and brought the little black box to life with light and sound. The Big Bopper crooned across the airwaves of one of her grandmother's favorite stations. Picking up her own glass and clinking it to Gabrielle's, she winked. "Like the refrigerator magnet says, I do love to cook with wine."

The women danced, sang, and broke another of Eve's rules by making a general mess of the kitchen. It felt good to relax and give way to abandon. There would be plenty of time to straighten up later.

Leaves whipped past the kitchen window and flew as quickly as the time. Soon the shadows of evening were threatening, and Gabrielle finally announced she had to leave. "I'm sorry, but I'm having dinner with the family. My brother is bringing his new girlfriend, and you know how my mother will be if I don't show."

"Take some cupcakes, and tell them I said hello." Eve packed the treats in a plastic container before handing them over. "Sneak them past Maria if you can." The last was said in reference to Gabrielle's mother and her failed attempts to keep Gabrielle's father on a diet. "I'll walk out with you."

With her scarf back in place to keep her hair from flying, Gabrielle linked arms with Eve, and the two headed out into the crisp autumn evening. It was early October, so the sun still peeked above the horizon, refusing to make way for the night. The trees went to bronze in the orange light, creating an idyllic setting as the women parted amidst promises to get together again.

Gabrielle backed out of the drive and zipped down the street in her little red convertible. Eve waved, then closed her eyes to enjoy the special smell that always accompanied the morphing of summer into fall. The heavy humidity that hung on through September had finally dissipated like a magic blanket.

There was something special about a small town where tradition was still king, and kids played until dusk. The people in the neighborhood were already expressing their love for the day of the dead with faux cobwebs and strands of orange pumpkin lights. Ghosts hung from trees while vampires and witches skulked on front porches. A cry of, "You're it!" caught her attention.

The boys laughing and tossing leaves around an imitation headstone didn't realize the scene they created. Or the memories they stirred for Eve. Icy spiders paraded across her shoulders, and she hugged herself. She pondered the innocence of children and hoped they would cling to it as long as possible.

With unhurried steps, she followed the paved walk, wondering how she would entertain herself the rest of the night. She was eager to get through tomorrow's proceedings and return to her carefully sculpted and controlled life. There were too many shadows in Pine Creek, and Eve never stayed for more than a few days.

No matter what happened, she had to be gone before Halloween.

Two

Trey Rainwater watched the women from his picture window as they said their good-byes. He recognized Gabrielle from town, so the tall blonde she was hugging had to be Eve Taylor. The woman he'd been waiting for.

After Gabrielle drove away, he continued to study Eve as she folded arms across her chest and basked in the setting sun. She turned her face into the wind as if breathing in the scent of life, allowing amber hair to fall in a wave over her shoulders.

He'd seen a few old pictures but was unprepared for the beauty she'd grown into. He'd been imagining a teenager with braids, nothing that would stir him to do anything more than he'd agreed, which was keep an eye on things and report what he deemed necessary.

The view of long legs in snug faded jeans made him revisit those plans.

The sweet drink of water next door was a full grown adult. What harm could come from getting to know her better? It would probably make his job that much easier in the process, if there turned out to be a job at all. That decision would fall to Eve, though she didn't know it yet.

Trey moved closer to the glass as Eve jerked her head toward something that caught her attention. He followed her line of sight to several young boys playing in a yard nearby. Her reaction to the carefree scene was unexpected and gave him pause.

As a Marine in Force Recon, Trey had often been the first

to locate an enemy camp. Missions had required stealth and attention to detail, practices that carried over to civilian life. He still watched people, noticing things others often missed, like the shadow of dread that flashed across Eve's face.

He recognized fear in the eyes of others, no matter how they tried to hide it. He glanced again at the kids then back to her. She was still staring, but with lips pursed now and delicate brows furrowed. Trey decided it was time to make his move.

A well-used brown leather jacket hung on a knob in the foyer, so he grabbed it to guard against the wind kicking up outside. Before he could make it to the door, repetitive beeps vibrated the cell phone lying on his desk.

"Sam," Trey said in answer, recognizing the name on the display. "What's up?" He slipped on the jacket as he listened to his friend suggest a weekend of fishing before the weather turned too cold. "I'll get back to you on that. The woman next door is around, so I'm going over. Yeah, that's the one."

Trey moved so he could see out the window and make sure Eve was still outside. She was there but walking back to the house. "Look, Sam. I'll call you later."

Eve was following the stone path toward her back door, but stopped and detoured to a large potted plant overturned in the yard. When she bent to shovel handfuls of soil back into the pot, Trey realized it was the opportune moment to meet his new neighbor.

Not really subterfuge. He'd just go over and lend a hand. Being chummy with neighbors wasn't usually his thing, since most people in his life were temporary, but this situation was different.

He was intrigued by her body language and mix of signals she broadcast, confidence slicked on top of uncertainty. Even from a distance he'd seen her tense up and couldn't help wondering what was roiling beneath the surface.

Pulling the door behind him, he stepped off the porch and made his way across the grass in her direction. Regardless of his own interest, Trey was beholden to make the leggy blonde's acquaintance. He'd made a promise to someone.

Someone Eve Taylor would never suspect.

~~~

Eve loved getting her hands dirty. The smell of freshly dug earth was something else she had missed since leaving home. No lawn or garden came with her little apartment. She could only lay claim to a few sprouts of bamboo wrapped in ribbon and two prickly cacti. Nothing else.

Gardening with her mother and grandmother had always been a favorite activity. Maybe she'd stopped growing plants because they reminded her of what she'd lost. What she'd left.

Eve studied her grandmother's yellow, two-story house. It was gracefully detailed with a strong skeleton built decades earlier. The home had withstood years of family gatherings and lover's quarrels, jelly-making at the end of summer and tornadoes come spring. It was everything an old southern home should be.

Inside, dark wood molding and floorboards punctuated colorful walls. Mint green, fresh-strawberry red, and butter cream made up the palette. A warm feeling of home and hearth tended to envelope whoever was lucky enough to spend time there. Friends and neighbors were always welcome to stop in unannounced, adding another layer to the rich history.

The large house had always been the centerpiece of a yard kept neatly trimmed but allowed to run wild with shrubs and creeping vines. *Mother nature will trim her handiwork when it's time.* She could hear her grandmother's words, and realized, as usual, Nan had known best. Plum trees were robust with their deep purple leaves, and the hardwoods had already given over their green to stronger, more vibrant colors of fall. It was a peaceful, welcoming place.

Eve cast her gaze back to the black dirt, intent on returning

it to the pot and hoping the task would help dispel her
melancholy. She hated being here, yet she loved it. She ached
for days spent on the porch sharing coffee and pie with her
family and stroking the old mutt that hung around because he
recognized a good thing.

She gripped the soil in her palms, hoping to squeeze out
regret and loneliness. "I had to go. They know I did." She had
no idea she'd spoken aloud until a voice startled her.

"Talking to the plant?"

Eve twisted her head around at the deep tone, unaware of
anyone's approach. The man had come across a lawn full of
leaves that should have given him away. "It's not a good idea
to sneak up on people." The sharp censure in her voice came
unexpectedly and made her bite her lip. "Especially when you
sneak so well."

The way he towered over her was unsettling, so she stood to
regain her composure and meet the stranger face to face. Her
five-foot-eight stature was usually the great equalizer. But not
this time.

At her full height with shoulders thrown back for added
benefit, he still had a good four inches on her. Four inches of
what was turning out to be a pleasant surprise.

The man held up his hands. "I didn't mean to scare you. I
just wanted to offer my condolences. Nan seemed like a nice
lady."

The kind sentiment contrasted with the dark look on his
face. Short black hair emphasized a strong jaw line and stern
brown eyes. If this man were a character in one of those popular
monster movies, he would definitely be on team werewolf. The
super hot kind of werewolf.

"You knew my grandmother?" Eve asked.

He swept his open palm through the air to indicate the
proximity of their houses. "We were neighbors."

"I'm sorry. What was your name?" Eve offered a hand then
realized it was still covered in dirt and dropped it. "I'm Eve

Taylor."

"I figured as much. Your grandmother talked about you often."

Eve didn't like being at a disadvantage. "Funny, she never mentioned you."

His eyes narrowed, almost imperceptibly. "Trey Rainwater. I've been here a few months, just renting."

"Rainwater? Native American?" That would explain the cheekbones and skin tone.

"Partially, yes. But the Rainwater name actually comes down from an English ancestor." Trey smiled and gave her a long, warm look from top to bottom and back again with no attempt to hide his approval. He was boldly and thoroughly checking her out.

Eve knew she should probably be insulted but was too busy trying to rein in her natural instincts. This man's masculinity was unavoidable and had various parts of her responding. A ten-ton truck of fierce-eyed, clean-shaven male had just laid her flat. Did aftershave usually smell that good?

She stumbled for something to say. "You're not a local, then?"

He motioned to the pot still lying on the ground then righted it with one hand. It would have taken both of Eve's arms and a good push from her thighs. Trey Rainwater was also packing some muscles under his brown jacket.

Dusting his hands, he shook his head and looked over her shoulder at nothing in particular. "No. I moved here from Arizona. This area was a good choice to start an office, and it's close to my parents. They're in North Carolina."

"An office? What business are you in?" Eve put her own dirty hands behind her back, wishing she had on a little makeup.

"I build websites." He said nothing more but held her gaze with an unwavering smile, one that was almost...predatory.

"You don't look like the computer whiz type." Eve wanted to suck the words back in. "I mean..."

Undaunted, Trey stood with hands in his pockets and feet

shoulder length apart. "Don't worry. I know what you meant. I may be a techie, but I know how to get dirty, too."

Eve simply gaped.

"I like to work on cars. As a hobby."

"Oh. Of course," Eve said, laughing and blushing in equal measure. "I've never met anyone who creates websites. I've played around with one of those templates but could never get it quite right. It always looked a little Romper Room when I put it all together. Maybe I could hire you, your company, I mean, to build one. If it's not too expensive."

She angled herself toward a nearby faucet and held up the hands that only moments before she had tried to hide. "Just going to wash off. Do you have a card on you?"

Dusting dirt from her fingers, Eve faced the side of the house so he wouldn't see her shut her eyes and grimace. She turned the red handle with a creak and let the water rush over her skin. It was freezing, but that was probably a good thing. She needed a distraction from Trey Rainwater and his overwhelming sexuality.

She was practically babbling already and needed to get it together. Men never made her react this way, like her nerve endings were on fire and electricity tingled in her chest. Maybe she should go back inside and hit some more of Gabrielle's wine.

"What kind of site do you need?"

She heard him moving closer and stood, one hand twisting the faucet until it dripped its last plaintive droplets. "I'm a caterer, at least I will be soon. I've got most of the information typed up, like menus, prices, about me. I need something basic and user friendly, classy but not intimidating."

She watched Trey as he closed the distance between them in a few long strides, his boots crunching on leaves. He wasn't moving quietly now. Had he meant to before?

Holding a blue card out to her, he used his other hand to shove a wallet into the back pocket of his jeans. *Lucky wallet.*

Eve surprised herself. Her mind was wandering down Lurid Street, and not one speck of guilt went with it.

She wiped her hands across the gray T-shirt she wore, not wanting to ruin the card. "Thanks. I'll look you up online and give you a call for a quote, if your stuff looks good."

A slow smile slid across his lips, and Eve melted.

"I'll do you a favor and won't even touch that one." His eyes lifted at the corners as if he were enjoying teasing her. "Call me when you're ready."

Eve crossed her arms over her chest like she always did when faced with a challenge. "I'll still want to check you out first."

He gave her that intensely personal once-over again, making her legs clench and her face burn. "You do that."

Eve enjoyed the view as he walked away, wondering what she had just encountered. His movements were easy and sure, like an animal lying in wait. Quiet, with a restrained energy that said, *Here, kitty, kitty. I won't bite.*

"Hmph." Eve tapped her foot. "I bet you do."

Why hadn't her grandmother told her about him? A man like Trey living next door would have been big news, and she was surprised Nan hadn't used the morsel of information to lure her back for a visit. Not that it would have worked.

Eve blew out a breath of regret. Trey Rainwater was a compelling man and left her filled with questions. His eyes had been wary but knowing, churning with a wealth of secrets.

Too bad she wouldn't be in town long enough to learn any of them.

~~~

The man drove with meticulous caution. Not too fast. Not too slow. He didn't want to draw any attention to himself. He'd waited until the mountains completely swallowed the sun before performing one of his drive-bys. Late night runs often helped him control his anger, so he let the windows down, allowing cool air to sweep in and calm the burning. He'd been waiting so long.

Fantasies and substitutions were all he'd had to get him through years of planning and waiting. The occasional trip to bigger cities gave him opportunities to exert some of his frustration on an unlucky hooker or a girl too strung out to realize what was happening, but those excursions were only for times of extreme desperation, when he knew he couldn't hold it in a minute longer.

He wouldn't have risked the little junkie last month if he'd known the course of things to come and how quickly things would change.

Sweat dampened his hands where he grasped the steering wheel. He was on the prowl, and the sensation coursed through his veins like a favored lover. The thrill of pursuit pushed him to a pulsing level of arousal, and there was only one thing in the world that could top that.

Hurting her.

He knew exactly what he would do when the time was right, and the dance of pinpricks across the back of his neck told him he was closer than ever.

He slowed to a creep as he drew near the house. The moon hovered high above, shedding pale blue light over the nighttime world. His world. A muted glow came from the upstairs windows, possibly a light in one of the back rooms. The old woman was dead, a lucky coincidence he couldn't have planned better himself, and the brother lived miles away. That left only one person who might be there, all alone in a house big enough to bury her screams.

Eve.

And she belonged to him.

THREE

The structural bones of downtown Pine Creek were much the same as they had been for the last hundred years. Main Street was still the central artery for a small town that pulsed slow and strong, knowing where it came from and where it wanted to go.

New businesses sprang up next to those that still had painted advertisements in their windows, but the city's architectural requirements allowed them to blend in a nicely diverse mosaic. The Law Offices of Hill and Dennis leaned toward the more classic design of stately brick with clean lines. It was on the sidewalk in front of this building that Eve waited for her brother, Lance. They were to meet here for the reading of their grandmother's will.

Nan had known Eve's parents would be fulfilling their retirement dream by traveling hundreds, if not thousands of miles from home. In consideration of that, she had stipulated that only Eve and Lance need be present for the reading.

Eve scanned the moderately busy street and tapped impatient fingers against her thigh. She was ready to get this entire ordeal over with. She would always remember her grandmother with love, and miss her every day, but the business end of death was even more depressing than the funeral had been. Having her grandmother's last wishes recited from a piece of paper seemed so cold and unattached.

A lime green Volkswagen bug honked as it passed, the driver waving to Eve. She didn't recognize the middle-aged woman behind the wheel but waved back anyway. With her family still residing here, people tended to remember Eve more than she did them. She often repressed memories associated with Pine Creek, a self-protecting habit she'd formed over the years.

Eve jumped when a hand fell on her shoulder.

"Hey, Mr. Crow," Lance said when Eve rounded on him. As children they had built a scarecrow to place among bales of hay for a fall yard display, and Eve had named the creature "Mr. Crow." With its long straw hair and stick legs, Lance had proclaimed it the likeness of Eve, a typical older brother cruelty. He still used the nickname.

"Hey, yourself. What took you so long?" Eve glanced at her watch to clarify how late he was.

"It's only ten after. I had to show a property and things ran over."

Eve smirked. "I don't suppose it was a female client?" Her brother was a walking advertisement for GQ magazine, bright blue eyes over a straight nose and mouth that always seemed on the verge of grinning. Women loved his blond, Nordic look, and Lance loved women. So no one left unhappy.

Straightening his tie, Lance pierced her with a look. "It was. A devastating beauty, Peanut Bowl Queen and everything. I couldn't rush out on such a promising business prospect."

"Anyone I know?" Eve asked with a wicked smile.

Pausing for effect, her brother whispered, "Alright, but can you keep a secret?" At Eve's nod he said, "Mrs. Langley is searching for the perfect place to stash her mother-in-law. It's going to be a surprise, for both her husband and his mother."

With a disappointed groan, Eve turned to push her way through the front door of the building, expecting Lance to follow. She was surprised to hear the sixtyish Mrs. Langley still had a mother-in-law.

A spicy scent of apples wafting from burning candles welcomed them as they entered. Comforting smells and elegant interior décor were meant to instill trust in the patrons that sought advice from the law firm. Heavy wood furniture spoke of reliability, while a fire snapping in the natural stone hearth put one at ease. Eve and Lance approached the young woman behind a massive desk and told her of their appointment.

The black-haired pixie gave Lance a flirtatious smile as she spoke into the phone, prompting Eve to step on her brother's toe in warning. "Don't even think about it," she mouthed.

Lance returned a patient sigh. "Fine, but watch the shoes."

Eve smothered a laugh just as a man emerged from a long hallway, his shoes clapping on hardwood floors. "Lance, good to see you." He shook hands with her brother before dazzling Eve with a lawyer's smile. "And you must be Eve. Nan spoke of you often."

He was the second stranger familiar with Eve because of her late grandmother. Guilt suddenly rose up and clogged her throat. It was evident Nan had missed her more than Eve ever realized. Had she been selfish to stay gone so long? She suddenly ached to hold her grandmother and apologize, to tell her she would stay if Nan needed her.

But the chance was gone.

"Ms. Taylor, are you feeling well?" The man's concern showed in the wrinkle of his brow. She estimated he was near her age, but chose to shave his head to disguise a receding hairline. A stocky torso stretched the sleeves of his suit and added to the tough guy persona, though his eyes were kind.

Eve cleared her throat. "I'm sorry. I must be a little preoccupied. It's a pleasure to meet you as well, Mr. Dennis."

Lance placed an arm around Eve's shoulders. "Do you want to do this later? I'm sure we can reschedule." He looked to the attorney for affirmation, but Eve spoke before he could respond.

"No. I'm fine. I'd really rather get it over with." She firmed her lips in what she hoped was a reassuring smile but couldn't shake the feeling that she'd let her family down. That she'd abandoned them. Her emotions had been in a riot since Nan's death, but remorse now reared its ugly head and blocked everything else.

She followed Mr. Dennis in silence as he traversed the labyrinth of halls. He opened a sturdy door with a gold plate reading "Kurt Dennis, Attorney at Law." He stood back, motioning for Eve and Lance to take seats in two plush navy armchairs facing his desk.

The lawyer seated himself across from them and opened a black file. "First off, please call me Kurt. Nan and I were on a first-name basis, and I feel like I already know both of you." He coughed and allowed a somber expression to settle on his face. "As you're aware, Nan asked if both of you could be present for the reading of her Last Will and Testament, as you are the primary beneficiaries. Since your mother was an only child, you have no cousins, and Nan's siblings are all deceased as well."

"What about our mother?" Eve broke in. "She receives the bulk of it, right?"

Kurt shrugged. "Nan and your mother worked things out between themselves. The portion allotted to your mother was separated from the estate before the will was drawn up."

"I see," Eve said, though she didn't understand at all. She glanced at Lance to gauge his reaction, but he stared straight ahead, avoiding eye contact with her. She nodded to Kurt. "Please go on."

"It's very cut and dried, really. Several belongings specified here," Kurt said as he slid a piece of paper across the desk to them, "are to go to Lance. Nan felt he had a sentimental attachment to them."

Lance scanned the list and smiled, then opened his eyes wide and pointed to the bottom of the document. "What is this figure?"

"That is the sum of your monetary inheritance." Kurt darted his eyes to Eve then down to the papers he shuffled in his hands.

Lance sat back in his chair. "I had no idea."

"Your grandmother was a shrewd investor." Keeping his

stare glued to the file in his hands, Kurt said, "Now as to you, Eve. A lesser sum has been bequeathed to you, as well as your grandmother's house and its belongings, minus those stipulated for your mother and Lance."

Eve gasped. "Why would she do that?" She turned to her brother. "You and Mom should take the house. It doesn't make any sense for me to have it."

"I'm afraid that won't be possible." Kurt's face was a display of consternation and discomfort. He let his mouth fall open, closed it then spoke quickly to Eve. "Your grandmother's wishes are very clear. You must take possession of the house immediately and maintain residency for one year. If you choose to do otherwise, the property and all its belongings will be sold and the proceeds donated to a charity of Nan's choosing."

Eve's head filled with a roaring static, her palms grew clammy, and the room spun. "I'm sorry. That's not possible. I can't live in that house. I can't live in Pine Creek, but that house must stay in our family. Surely there's an alternative."

Kurt shook his head as if it had grown heavy. "There is none. Any attempt to circumnavigate the terms will result in forfeiture of the property."

"What does that mean?" She was clenching the navy leather arms of the chair now, and sitting forward like a runner at his mark. "I can just sign the house over to Mom, right?"

Lance placed a hand over Eve's. "That would be the circumnavigating part."

One look at her brother and Eve knew. "You were aware of this all along, weren't you? How could you not prepare me for this?"

"I didn't know specifics. Mom told me that you weren't going to be happy after today, but she and Nan felt it was in your best interests." Lance gave his attention to the paper he still held that listed his portion of the estate. "I'm sorry, I didn't know it would be this extreme."

Eve sprang from her chair. "I don't care about the money.

What about my life? My sanity? I had plans in another city and state entirely. Now I'm either trapped in..." she couldn't form the words, "in ..this...this place, or I'll have to be responsible for losing Nan's house. That house has been in our family for over eighty years!"

"So what are you going to do? It's only a year of your life." Lance stood to face off with his sister. "You can start your business here as easily as you can anywhere else. In fact, it will probably take off in Pine Creek. You have contacts here, and there's a college town just up the road."

"That's not the only issue, and you know it." Eve pressed her lips together, afraid of what she might say next. The walls of the lavish office were starting to pound at her. She felt like she was in a very swanky, yet overheated coffin. "I'm sorry, Mr. Dennis. I have to take a moment and think about this. I need some air."

Eve was already opening the door when Kurt called after her, "I need to know by this evening. You'll have to sign these papers!"

Eve barreled toward the lobby, intent on breathing in the fresh air outside. She couldn't think in here, the place where she'd been ambushed by loved ones. "He needs to know by tonight?" she grumbled to herself. "I guess Nan didn't want to leave me any time to wiggle out of this."

With controlled steps, she marched out the door of the firm and looked both ways up and down the street. She had no idea where to go, who to talk to. And she needed to talk. Gabrielle was not an option. Deep down, Eve knew her friend would side with her family. They all thought Eve's avoidance of Pine Creek had stolen pieces of her life. That it was the controlling factor in all her choices.

Deciding to get a strawberry shake from old Mr. Mason's ice cream shop, she headed in that direction with her hands clasped together and her purse clutched under one arm. Her fingers tingled from being clamped so tightly, so she relaxed and imagined getting the shake to go. She would park herself on a bench beneath the trees and sort this mess out.

Rounding a corner, she came to a dead stop at the sight that greeted her. The side of the building displayed centuries old brick, but the front had been turned into a glass-paneled wall from the ground level up to the third floor. She remembered it being a department store that had gone out of business. It had been empty for years but now offered passers-by a glimpse of sleek, contemporary offices. Through the glass she could see people moving about modern work spaces and bursts of colorful artwork on light gray walls.

Somehow, she wasn't surprised to see the name on the storefront. Rainwater Site Design. "Well, well. It looks like my neighbor wasn't overstating himself at all."

Eve slid her hand over the French braid of her hair. The turmoil that had tracked her since leaving the lawyer and Lance behind was gone. She actually thought of Trey Rainwater as her neighbor and didn't flinch in response. She couldn't possibly be accepting her new conditions already, could she?

Whatever the reason, she felt calmer and came to the conclusion Trey was who she could talk to. He was completely removed from the issue and would offer an objective opinion. He'd certainly struck her as a man who wouldn't hold back on account of her feelings. That was exactly what she needed. Someone who didn't care about her and wouldn't let prickly emotions get in the way of the truth. Whatever that may be.

A man noticed Eve immediately and spread a bright smile across his lips. "Can I help you?"

"I'm looking for Mr. Rainwater. He's not expecting me, but..." Eve stopped, catching sight of the man himself coming down a metal staircase. He wore black pants and shirt, both professional, yet unable to hide the broad shoulders and lean torso beneath. He approached her with a sinful lift of one eyebrow. "Eve. You said you would call."

His deep chocolate eyes settled on hers, and Eve's heart gave one long squeeze before resuming its natural rhythm. "I know this is unexpected, but I was hoping we could talk."

"Come up to my office."

Eve put a hand on his arm to stop his movement. "Wait. Somewhere else?" She was afraid she might get emotional and didn't want to do so in his workplace.

He studied her as she bit her lip and held her breath then called over his shoulder to the ponytailed man at the reception desk. "John, I'm going out."

Four

"Your usual, Mr. Rainwater?" asked an eager-to-please boy behind the counter.

Trey nodded. "Medium, black." He looked at Eve. "What for you?"

Smooth jazz lingered in the aromatic coffee shop called Brown Beans, one of Trey's daily stops, though this visit made twice in one day. Orange and cocoa walls warmed the environment and called to pedestrians to come in for a shot of caffeine-induced bliss. He was surprised how busy the store was, late for breakfast yet not quite lunch.

"I was in the mood for ice cream, but a venti cafe mocha sounds good. No whipped cream," Eve told the boy who now turned his rapt attention to the stunning woman. Her soft smile brought a blush to his young, freckled face.

Trey studied Eve's profile as she continued to chat. Her nose sloped gently over full, pink lips, tempting in their expressiveness. When she'd walked into his business earlier, he'd once again been struck by her eyes. Light blue and flecked with gold, they were framed by straight brows that lent a degree of edginess to an otherwise angelic face.

When she turned those eyes back to him, Trey almost put one hand on the small of her back before thinking better of it. Such an intimate gesture might bother her. Hell, it bothered him that he felt the impulse.

Shoving payment for their drinks across the counter, he spoke gruffly. "Keep the change," he said, surprising both Eve and the barista in training who nodded with wide eyes and started making their coffees as if his life depended on it.

Eve pressed her lips together, probably restraining a comment on his rudeness. Well, she had sought him out, so if he offended her, too damn bad. "You wanted to talk?" he asked, turning his back on her and heading for a secluded seating area. He was intent on smothering the chivalry that had reached up to choke him before.

He sat in a hard-backed chair just as Eve settled herself into an explosion of burgundy velvet that belonged in a harem. "I wanted some advice, even the hard cold truth. Looks like I came to the right person," she said in a clipped voice.

"Are we talking about your website?" he asked, doubtful that was the reason since they weren't having this conversation in his office.

She sipped her frothy drink before answering. "I've got a problem and need an objective opinion. I don't visit Pine Creek often, and when I do it's in short bursts. I have my own reasons for avoiding the town, which I'd rather not go into. Just know I have a serious aversion to being here."

"Noted." Trey kept his comments to a minimum, well aware that silence encouraged confession. He thought he knew what was coming next whether he wanted to be her chosen confidant or not.

"My grandmother left me her house," Eve announced as if he should be shocked by such a revelation. "I have to move in or it will be sold off, like some unwanted junk at a yard sale. The house where my mother grew up."

Trey carefully arranged his features into bland apathy. "So move in."

"How can you jump to that conclusion? You don't know the half of it."

"Because you're only telling me half, and with the information I have so far, my advice is to move into the house." He took the opportunity to sip his coffee as she stared at him as she would a two-headed dog. "Other than not liking the town, what's keeping you...wherever it is that you live now? Do you need to sell your own place first, or does it have something to do with your catering?" He tilted his head. "A man?"

Eve curled her lip. "No. Nothing is permanent there. I guess I'm like you in that aspect. Just renting."

"Then I don't see any reason for you to stay away. In fact, I don't understand why you haven't come back more often. It seems like you and your grandmother were close, and I know she missed you."

He could see Eve's invisible armor falling into place. "What do you know about it? You were her neighbor for less than a year. Nan and I kept in touch, and our relationship was strong. We understood each other."

"Maybe that's why she left you the house."

Trey's simple statement deflated her defensiveness, and he watched her shoulders slump while anger and confusion battled in her eyes. She heard the truth in his words, and was probably acknowledging her grandmother would never have done anything to hurt her. That Nan knew all along what Eve would do. What she needed, even if Eve couldn't admit it to herself.

"I don't have a choice," she said with acceptance. "Losing the house would be losing what's left of my childhood."

He chose not to probe further into her last statement, though Nan had made similar comments about Eve as a child and realities she should never have seen. Her past was in there somewhere, and he would have time to dig it out. Time to find out what secret tore at the woman across from him. If she stayed, and Trey suspected she would.

Conflict ate at his gut. He had an obligation to fulfill, and it would require omitting details from Eve. For reasons he couldn't explain and didn't want to analyze, the idea of holding the truth from her was disturbing. He found himself involved on an entirely different level than he'd prepared for.

She was a golden siren, calling to him to move closer yet quick to coil and strike when cornered. She managed to tantalize and perplex at once, though he doubted either was intentional.

Trey softened his tone but laced his words with the steel he knew she needed from him. "So you'll do what has to be done. You've made the decision, now execute."

An unexpected smile tugged at her lips. "You were military," she stated with certainty. "Should have known."

The look she gave him was a mix of admiration and trust that shot a bolt of heat through his veins, making him want to pull her from the ridiculous chair and onto his lap. She was blithely unaware of the door she'd just opened. The invitation he would willingly accept.

"Eve, is that you? I heard you were in town." Eve and Trey turned their heads simultaneously to see a vivacious woman streamlining toward them. Amanda "Mandy" Pickerson had them in her sights and was moving in. Her brown-hair, streaked with blonde, bounced at the edges with every step she took.

Eve looked as shell-shocked as Trey felt. "Mandy, hi. How are you?"

"Good, good." Mandy pulled up a chair before she bothered to ask, "Mind if I join you?" She gave a stilted nod in Trey's direction. "Trey." Then she put the force of her attention back on Eve. "I can't believe the good fortune of running into you here. I was just talking to Joanne Stevens the other day about you and the family. Sorry to hear about your grandmother, by the way."

Trey snorted, assuming that was the perky version of condolence. He was ignored.

"You know I'm working over at The Herald. They still haven't changed that unoriginal name, but what can you do?"

Eve nodded, though the tension around her eyes betrayed her. She wanted to bolt.

No one encouraged her, but Mandy continued after a quick

breath. "Anyway, I have my own column now, a mix of society and current news, and I wanted to interview you about your new venture. Joanne said you were opening up a restaurant or something?"

Eve shook herself and glanced to Trey with pleading eyes.

"Why not?" he said. "Why don't you tell her all about it. Where you'll be based." He threw the dare at Eve's feet, wanting to see how she would perform under pressure.

Her eyes took on a blaze like turquoise in the sun, brows arching in recognition of the challenge and acceptance. She cocked her head to Mandy. "Actually, I'll be moving back to Pine Creek to start up."

"Really?"

Trey would swear the reporter's hair bounced of its own accord. She reached down to hoist a large red bag onto her lap and was pulling out a pad and pen when a woolly head popped out and growled.

Eve jumped. "What is that?"

"A dog," Mandy cooed, pouting her lips and stroking the little brown head that bore an unconvincing sunflower bow. She put the bag back down between herself and Eve, prompting the furry bow to growl again.

"How sweet," Eve muttered, though she crossed her legs away from the animal in case it went for flesh.

"So you'll do the interview?" Mandy beamed at Eve. "I promise it will get you lots of attention."

Trey felt more than he saw the deep breath Eve took before opening her mouth and leaping into commitment. "Sure. I'll take free advertising."

As Mandy flipped open her book, Trey rose from his chair, already regretting the loss of time spent in Eve's company. Mandy was gearing up, and when Eve rounded her lips in question, he shrugged without apology. "Glad I could help."

Eve's stare called him a coward and followed him out of the coffee shop. A rumble of laughter rolled deep in his chest. He was sure he'd be hearing all about how much Eve appreciated being left alone with the little pit bull.

And her dog.

He raised his cup in salute as he passed the front window, then faced the sidewalk that would lead him back to work, a grin still quirking his lips. Yeah, he'd be hearing all about it.

From his brand new neighbor.

~~~

On the heels of her interview with Mandy, Eve practically speed-walked back to Kurt Dennis to sign the papers, doing the very thing she had mentally accused her grandmother of earlier. Leaving no time to wiggle out of the decision she'd made.

So what if she turned her head from every Halloween decoration she passed on the way? One crisis at a time.

Getting away from the lawyer, and the piece of paper she felt might as well have been signed in blood, was just as crucial. Hounds of nausea and shock still nipped at her heels as she strolled the quaint streets downtown, reeling from the inescapable reality that she was home again. For good.

A distraction was what was called for. Something to redirect the adrenaline currently making a mockery of the bravado she had shown in the coffee shop.

She needed to immerse herself in the one thing that would ease the butterflies fluttering...no, that was all wrong...the dragons swooping and diving in her stomach. The ones torching her insides with what were surely flames of madness, since despite having no real alternative, her decision to relocate to Pine Creek, for an entire year, was nothing short of straight-jacket behavior.

So she channeled her bottled up energy and hit every home improvement and appliance store in a twenty mile radius. Nothing soothed a cook's soul like a browse through cutlery, spice racks, ranges, and refrigerators. Many women preferred diamonds, but Eve would give her heart to the man wise enough to bring her a hammered egg-white bowl.

The sky was dark when she walked out of the last specialty shop and drove home in a car loaded with swatches, tile samples, and magazines. The first phase of Operation Dream Kitchen was in effect, and she had no doubt Nan would approve the use of Eve's small monetary inheritance for the purpose.

A sweet surprise awaited her on the porch. Her porch. That was something that would take getting used to.

A peace lily rested by the front door in a shiny blue ceramic pot. Eve knew before looking at the card who it was from. Her brother always bought flowers when he felt guilty.

Hurrying to get out of the bracing wind, she hauled the shopping bags into the house and positioned her housewarming gift in the foyer. She would call Lance and clear the air then whip up something to eat before diving into the decorating magazines.

After all, a great kitchen was more than just chrome and gloss. Colors and patterns reflected personalities, either of the individual or a family as a whole. From neat as a pin bachelor nooks and pop-art stools to crowded cucinas with scratched wooden tables.

Kitchens kept a home alive with morning pancakes in the air, sandwich fixings for a midnight snack, you-wash-I'll-dry conversations, and most importantly, a gathering place for the moments you remembered the rest of your life. Even if you couldn't recall the details. You never forgot the love.

Caught in an ever-changing daydream of how she would put it all together, Eve was caught off guard by a metallic ring that filled the house with calamity. It couldn't be her cell phone, since it was emitting from multiple locations.

Her gaze fell on one of the culprits that hung on the wall by the refrigerator. "My God...a land line. I almost forgot what those sounded like."

Laughing at herself, she answered the yellow clunker. "Hello?"

"Yes, I'm calling for Eve Taylor," said a female voice over the line.

"This is she." Eve studied the old dial on the base of the phone, but it couldn't tell her who was calling.

"This is Miranda Hay. I didn't have your personal number, so I thought I'd try your grandmother's. Guess I was right," she said with a smile in her voice.

Eve held a picture in her head of a woman with long brown hair and a denim skirt, older by a few years and always cheerful. "You were. It's nice to hear from you."

"It's been floating around the pumpkin patch that you're doing some catering."

Eve's mouth fell open. The Internet had nothing on small town gossip. "Well, I'm not up and running yet."

"That's fine. Just fine. My little boy, Deke, will be eight in December, and I want to plan a special party. Will that be enough time?"

Eve could hear Miranda's breath being held in anticipation. It was her first official client. How could she refuse? Plus, no one spread the word better than busy mothers, and a good client referral was worth its weight in lasagna. "I can pull that off. What did you have I mind?"

"I was hoping you could help with that. I'm not terribly creative, but it needs to be the polar opposite of anything to do with Christmas. We like to keep it as separate as we can."

Eve put a finger to her lip. "Hmmm...makes me think summer, but it will be chilly in December. We need something that will serve both purposes. Kids love being outdoors, and bonfires always go over well."

"Like a barbecue?"

An idea hit. "How about a winter Luau? We can adjust dress and activities so they reflect the theme. Cold weather versions."

"Oh. I'm so excited! I knew you'd be the jackpot. Let me

know what you need from me, and price is no object, well, within reason." The woman's glee almost came through the mouthpiece.

"No worries there, and I'll be in touch."

After hanging up, Eve did a little twirl and jiggle, throwing in a couple of jumps to get it out. "My first client, with no advertising expense at all." She sashayed to the drawer where she knew the phone book was kept. A celebratory pepperoni with extra cheese pizza was in order, and this was one of those times when it was okay to let another do the cooking.

Still pleased with herself, her words practically hummed in the silent house. "And I haven't even opened for business."

That brought her up short. She hadn't opened because she wasn't ready. Business cards, menu options, license. Those were just the tip of the ice sculpture, not to mention she still had to move out of her apartment.

She looked at the stack of samples again. Time was suddenly her worst enemy. She needed at least a week for perusing slate or marble countertops, cold storage options, utensils, bowls, packaging, delivery. She was giving herself a headache.

Slow. Steady. Two things must be done first.

First a phone call to let Gabrielle know what was happening and that backup was needed. This she did while opening a brand new bag of café mocha coffee. The second necessity, lots of caffeinated encouragement.

Gabrielle would still be out of the local hearsay loop, having been at her shop all day, and in the next town. She was in for a shock.

When her friend answered, Eve launched into a synopsis of the day's events, including a snippet regarding Trey Rainwater. She held back on that topic, ensuring Gabrielle's firecracker of a car would be screeching to a halt outside to nudge the pizza delivery guy out of first place.

As the coffee brewed and Eve fantasized, a small but determined spark of joy ignited in a place she never knew existed. Where no timidity or doubt lurked to spoil the party. What an unexpected, thrilling, roller-coaster ride she'd been on the last ten hours.

And here she had landed, all because of an eight-year-old's birthday party.

Spirit soaring and expectations blooming, Eve danced around the kitchen, doing her own version of the mambo with a tape measure for partner. Fortune really must be a woman, because she felt blessed. On top of the stars.

She was so happy, she forgot to be scared.

FIVE

Eve noticed two things upon opening the front door. First, the paperboy threw awfully short, making her glad for the red-silk robe she'd hastily thrown on. With the wealth of her legs exposed, she still made it a quick dash to the front yard and back. All the neighbors would see was the jewel-eyed dragon on her back as she bent for The Herald then hurried for cover.

The second thing was an envelope, orange, the size of a thank you note or party invitation, and lying squarely on the mat. No name. How did she miss it last night?

Scooping it up as well, she closed out the cold and headed for the steaming cup of coffee she'd left in the kitchen. More interested in the card, she let the unrolled paper drop carelessly on the wooden island while she tore open the envelope. Inside, a single note of the same pumpkin color slid out onto the counter. She unfolded it and found a poem.

> *You are full fair 'tis true*
> *No ebony hair*
> *Or skin so fair*
> *Can compare to you*

Odd, it made little sense, not quite romantic, but teasing and a little ominous.

Of course. It must belong to Gabrielle. Eve would call and let her know she'd dropped it on the way out. Probably from one of the customers that frequented the shop Gabrielle owned.

Mystics. The name said it all.

Oh yeah. It all made sense now. The card and poem lined up perfectly with some of the characters who browsed there. They were interested in crystals, candles, and spells, and this poem would fit right in.

Relieved to have a somewhat plausible answer, Eve redirected her thoughts to the kitchen design she and Gabrielle had knocked out the night before. It would be gorgeous and just her style. Shopping would reign again today, but this time she'd be bringing more than ideas home. She couldn't wait.

Canon in D sounded in her purse, surprising her enough to spill a scalding drop on her hand before she grabbed the phone from its pocket. "Hello?" She worried about any call so early in the morning.

"Eve, are you okay?" It was Lance, his tone tense and laced with concern.

Eve responded wryly, "Yeah, somehow I managed to make it through the night, but I am being harassed by pre-breakfast phone calls. What's going on?"

The doorbell rang, prompting Eve to cut him off. "Hold on. Someone's at the door. Why is this place Grand Central before I've even had my first cup?"

"Eve, wait, I need to tell you something."

Her brother's words registered as she cracked the door to see Trey standing outside, grim-faced with arms folded. "Hold on, Lance."

"A little early for visits, you think?" she said to Trey, keeping her body hidden behind the heavy wood, still covered in nothing but the short robe.

"Can I come in? We need to talk." He moved forward, forcing Eve to open and let him in. His eyes flickered to her legs long enough to tell her he noticed them before he brushed past her.

"Good morning to you, too. And please make yourself at home," she said, sarcasm shooting daggers at his back.

Using outrage for a shield, she refused to feel uncomfortable with her state of undress. His familiarity with the inside of the house was apparent as he headed straight for the kitchen. So he'd been here before to visit Nan. Well, it was her damn house now.

"Maybe I gave you the wrong impression yesterday." Eve folded her arms across her chest and followed. "I appreciate the pep talk and realize we're going to be living next door to each other, but you can't just barge in here whenever you like."

The hand he held up to still her tirade was firm and unyielding. "I said we need to talk." He looked at the phone dangling from her hand, bringing her attention back to the call she'd been ignoring.

"Lance, you still there? What did you want to tell me, but be quick. I've got something here I need to deal with." A fulminating glare at Trey backed up the statement.

"No, I haven't read it yet." She reached for the newspaper, but Trey snatched it from beneath her grasp. "What the hell is going on?" she asked of both men.

"Who's with you?" her brother asked over the line.

"A friend." Measuring the determination in Trey's stance, she told Lance, "Whatever it is, I'll be fine. Thanks for the heads-up." She hung up before her brother could argue.

"Either let me see it or spill," she told the man standing across from her, The Herald still wrapped up in his hand.

He opened the paper and tossed it on the island between them. "Mandy's article. It's not about catering."

The coil of dread in her stomach was back. She'd almost made it a whole twenty-four hours without it.

"What is it about?" she asked, eyeing the paper as if it were a dead animal, then scooping it up to read the headlines. "I don't see it." Pages rustled harshly before she spotted the title. She knew instantly it referred to her and went straight to page 3B.

Eve read out loud, "Survivor Comes Home," then snorted. "She's less than creative if that's supposed to grab attention. Makes me sound like a war hero." Eve cringed inwardly when realization hit. "Did you read it?" Though she knew he had.

"Yes."

"I don't want to talk about it. I'm too churned up and might take it out on you." She downed the last of her coffee and stalked to the pot to pour another. "Want some?" she asked, then grabbed a black cup, because it suited him, and filled it. He accepted it with no further comment.

Eve's hands clenched the edge of the counter. "I really want to use a word that is unladylike. How is it you're always catching me at my worst moments?"

Trey only smiled and sipped, making her study him harder for signs of a reaction. She hadn't wanted him to know. There was too much that went along with her past, and talking about any part of it might loosen her lips more than she wanted. He had been friendly thus far, but she didn't really know anything about him. How would he behave now, knowing she was damaged goods?

Eve let her eyes run over Trey's lean torso as he rested himself against the wall. Even with all the drama and distraction, she managed to appreciate the snug fabric across broad shoulders. Relaxed and sipping a steaming mug, he fit right in, and she didn't mind sharing the space as much as she normally might. Historically, she liked her alone time and her privacy.

She blew out a breath. The most private and damaging moment of her life had just been broadcast to the county, dragging it all up again. Why would anyone care? It was ancient history.

Finally breaking the silence, Trey nudged her with his elbow. "I can't call her that particular word either, because I was raised to believe it's degrading to women."

Eve curved her lips half-heartedly.

"But if it makes you feel any better," he added, "I'm thinking it real hard."

~~~

Trey got what he wanted when Eve's un-painted, yet still-alluring mouth, broke into a grin. The compulsion to comfort her had hit as soon as he'd read Mandy's article. It gave him new insight into Eve's resistance to living in a place where such atrocities had occurred.

Where they had happened to her.

Trey understood her defensiveness and wished he'd known all along. He hadn't been told the whole story, so he'd derided her for staying gone, believing her to be selfish. He had pushed her without realizing the demons she faced in Pine Creek.

He wouldn't say he regretted it, playing a role in her decision to accept the house and brave out an entire year. But that added to his other agenda...well, he would have to do what he could to help her out now. He owed her something.

Trey nursed the inkling of guilt, seeing the wisdom of focusing on it instead of other emotions. Especially with Eve standing there half-naked and glorious in her rage.

In his rush to intercept the article and break the news himself, he hadn't considered the hour of the day or how she might be dressed. Maintaining his integrity was growing more difficult by the minute, with her golden legs bared to mid-thigh and hair tousled by sleep. Fury colored her cheeks, and he imagined other situations that might bring that flush to her face.

There I go again. Failure to repair. Trey pulled himself back in.

"I know you don't want to talk about it," he began. The look she flashed him was a warning. "But I wanted to apologize. I didn't know your reason for avoiding this place, and I never would have encouraged you to talk to Mandy if I had." He sighed. "I should have known. She doesn't have a reputation for compassion."

Eve shrugged then walked over to lean against the wall beside him. For a moment they both reveled in a mutual agreement to be silent.

Trey noticed her toenails were painted a murderous red.

He asked the question that drilled at him. "Will this change your mind?" He wasn't really involved, so why did he hold his breath while waiting for her answer?

Eve pointed to the wooden work table. "I'm thinking about keeping that. It's such a unique old piece, and you can't get an island with that much space. It doesn't have a lot of storage beneath, but I like it. It could blend."

Trey said what he knew she was thinking. "And that's where you and Nan cooked together."

She nodded, looking right through the table as if seeing herself at a younger age. "It's where I learned, at her elbow, to love it." Eve gave a short laugh. "The culinary gene skipped a generation, and since my mom never showed any interest, Nan showered all of her knowledge on me."

"So when do I get to taste some of that knowledge?"

Eve tossed a glance his way, a wary wrinkle on her forehead as if searching for double meaning in what he'd said, then she retreated to the sink to wash her cup. "Not today. I've got work to do." Turning her back on him she tightened the robe's belt and strode away.

He would swear she sauntered out of the room that way on purpose but couldn't complain about the effect it had on him. He needed his blood warmed before facing the cold outside.

Eve poked her head back around the doorjamb and smiled. "But if you're available, I might need a strong back later." Then she was gone.

Trey listened to the sound of footsteps on the stairs, movement above, then the rush of running water. She was taking a shower.

The movie now playing in his head was just too explicit. Tortuous. It involved sudsy water rolling over bare curves, so he put his cup in the sink and headed for the door, purposely leaving his jacket draped on his arm.

He had been wrong before. The bracing wind would probably turn out to be a good thing, because his blood had suddenly gotten too damn warm.

~~~

He liked them young. There was a certain tug and pull to skin that still had so much life in it. Blood was a different color, too, he would swear. Richer and sweeter to smell.

The girl had been in the library for hours, studying for one of the tough exams for her pre-med major. Little sweetheart wanted to be a doctor.

She should know something about the body's response to pain then. Good. Maybe she'd teach him a thing or two in trade for some restraint on his part. Though holding back wouldn't alter the end result.

She didn't know her fate was in his hands tonight. The only thing running through her mind was cellular biology or some such thing, making her feel smarter than average. He sneered.

Or she could be imagining her fraternity boyfriend, wishing she had time for a quickie before heading back to her dorm. Whore. She probably used her looks to get whatever she wanted and would try to use those tricks on him. She would try to get away.

But no one got away from him. Ever. That was a mistake he wouldn't repeat. It had cost him too much before.

A silhouette crossed one of the curtain-free windows. He couldn't make out details but knew it was her. He'd been watching her for days and knew the shape of her body from every direction. Petite and slim with black hair in an ever-present braid down her back. She'd be wearing that damn crucifix too, good Catholic that she was.

He wasn't fooled.

She would be surprised at first, then terrified when the rag pressed over her nose and mouth. She would struggle for less than a minute, the rapid beat of a frantic heart speeding up the effects of his drug.

He stepped out into the shadow cast by a giant tree, invisible to prying eyes, and rounded the back of his truck in time to meet her. Head down as she scrounged in her purse, the young woman came up short when her toes stepped on his. Big blue eyes widened before she spoke. "Oh, sorry. I didn't see you."

"You never have," he said as one arm locked her and the books she carried in a vise. He covered her face with his free hand, so the startled scream couldn't penetrate the cloth. He crushed her lips without mercy.

During the brief struggle, he wondered if she knew what was coming. She would know the typical dangers facing a college coed and that harm was just as likely to come from the sweet-faced guy in algebra as it was a complete stranger.

She might assume he would take her off somewhere and slap her around a little, maybe force a gun to her head or a knife to her throat as he fed off her fear. Or she could be expecting to be tied down and raped, perhaps repeatedly. Such common crimes were all over the news.

The man slid the girl's limp form behind his seats and smiled to himself. People had so little imagination.

Six

It was amazing what you could get done in only a few days when you knew the right people and had a plan. Eve was in on both counts. She'd pulled a few of her grandmother's strings as well as one of her own to get the renovations started and would soon be cooking in a brand new kitchen.

She almost felt guilty re-doing Nan's house but remembered how often the older woman had mentioned the urge to do the very same thing. Except she'd always said she would wait for Eve, because she wanted her to have a hand in it.

Eve wondered now if her grandmother had left the job undone on purpose. Perhaps it was a parting gift meant to soothe the transition back to Pine Creek. It would be like Nan to do that. Leave her stuck in the house, but with a project Eve would love to throw herself into and the finances to really have fun with it.

Although calling it fun wasn't quite accurate. She was in chef utopia.

With a proud and anticipatory grin, Eve spun in a slow circle to assess the work that had been completed and envision what was left to be done. New cabinets had been hung to provide plenty of storage. Two sets had glass panes to showcase earthy green and beige dishware. It would be a place of business for her, but still a home to be admired. The ivory color of the cabinetry was a lovely classic style that contrasted against the deep brown granite countertops and hardwood floor running throughout the house.

Her grandmother's wooden table was still intact, too. Well,

mostly. The large butcher-block island had been re-sealed to bring out the wood's natural warmth, but its sturdy square legs had been painted a nice cream to match the cabinets as well as the bead board façade that enclosed the open area beneath the table. Shelving inside would allow for even more storage, one thing a cook could never have enough of.

Eve tapped her fingernails against the stone tiled backsplash, also an eggshell color with brown speckles that lent it an antique feel. The same stonework had been used behind the gaping hole where the gas range would be housed. Right next to the pot filler faucet. No more wrestling with large pots and spilling half the pasta. There was still a classic faucet set in the deep farmhouse sink that would be more than roomy enough for the mounds of dirty dishes she couldn't wait to create.

Now she just needed the stainless steel appliances to arrive, and she would be in business. The new refrigerator had two drawers for freezer foods, she had to have a gas range, and of course there would be a double oven. These were the necessities. The French burner that came in the middle of the range as well as the steam oven, speed ovens and warming drawer, those were plain old indulgence.

And there was still shopping left to do.

Movement outside brought her toward the window to investigate. It seemed there had been a flash of brown in her yard, so she headed to the front parlor and peeked through the vertical blinds.

Someone out there alright. Trey was stepping up onto her porch now, wearing the jacket he'd had on when they first met. The one that made him look all rough and male, enticing in a way that had Eve wanting to slide her hands beneath and bury her face in his neck to enjoy the mix of man and leather.

His knock grounded her in reality. She hadn't talked to him since the day Mandy's article had surfaced. Granted, she had been caught up in renovations and too busy to see him, but he hadn't made any attempt either.

It was a surprise to see him now, and Eve realized he had pulled back, giving her space. It was considerate but also expected, given his feelings about commitment. If he desired constant change of scenery, women were probably included in the package.

Scoffing to herself, Eve pursed her lips. They hadn't even kissed, so it wasn't like she was falling into the yesterday's news category.

A breeze rushed in through the cracked door, brushing her hair back from her face and bringing the scent of Trey with it. Liquid warmth gathered in her belly when he lifted one corner of his mouth. His dark eyes zeroed in on her with no hesitation. Here was a man who took what he wanted.

"Come in. It's cold out there," Eve muttered, unnerved by the detour her thoughts took when he was around. Maybe she should just jump on him and get it over with, but the sensation of having him pursue her was just too good to sacrifice. He was not the kind of man to be led anywhere, and Eve's secret inner female enjoyed his cocksure attitude.

Trey was like a new and untried recipe. She'd have to wait for the end result, not knowing what she'd find when it was done. But anticipation was half the pleasure.

"I think I have something you want," Trey said.

Damn, was he reading her mind? "Okay," Eve answered with a smile intended to be alluring. She wasn't usually one to play the vamp, but euphoria from decorating still lingered. She also had a desire to taste the shadow of stubble along Trey's jaw.

"A van."

Her ego deflated. "Sorry, what?" She gathered the wits that had briefly scattered. "Oh, I do need some sort of transportation for jobs, but I was going to get by with Lance's Rover until I could afford something of my own."

Trey looked past her to the calamity in the kitchen. "Coming along." He pulled a piece of paper from his pocket and unfolded it to show her a picture of a white van. "This is what it will look like when it's done."

"Done with what?" Eve asked skeptically.

Taking her by the hand, Trey led her to the living room and pulled her down beside him on the floral sofa her grandmother had kept way past its prime. Eve already had her eye on its replacement, but further redecorating would have to wait.

He flipped the paper over and pointed to some designs scratched in pencil below notes written in what she assumed was his handwriting. She'd like to hear an analysis of those blocky letters and what it would tell her about the enigmatic man who sat beside her, scorching her thigh whenever his leg accidentally rubbed hers. "I can get the vehicle cheap. It's not that old but has some body damage."

"What's your version of cheap?" Eve asked.

He gave her a number that started the gears clicking in her head. She could afford it. "I'll still have to pay for body work. Can't show up to jobs in a car that reflects badly." She knew his business mind would understand what she meant.

"Which is why I'm offering to take care of that for you. Consider it a welcome-to-the-neighborhood gift."

Eve sat back and considered his offer. It would be a great help and would move her along even faster. "I'll have to pay you something."

Trey lifted one shoulder. "We'll work it out in trade."

Eve's eyes widened and blinked in surprise, causing a harsh sound to escape from his lips. "I'll need some affairs catered throughout the year, and will gladly seek repayment in full."

"Hm." Eve looked away, mildly embarrassed by her quick judgment and the fact he'd picked up on it.

A firm hand on the back of her neck brought her back to face him. "That's one thing I won't buy or trade for. I give us both more credit than that." His mouth was on hers before she could speak, surprisingly gentle but insistent as he moved against her.

Eve's senses responded in full, and she slid her arms over his shoulders, moving closer, needing contact with the heat of his chest. She felt his other hand move to the hollow of her throat and linger hesitantly before he pulled away, leaving her cold and empty.

"Sorry, I didn't plan that." Trey stood and stuffed his hands in his jean pockets to secure them.

Dazed, Eve lifted her fingers to the spot on her neck where she could still feel the touch of his hand and her pulse throbbing in response. "Me, either."

After a few shaky breaths, she regained her composure and dragged her eyes up to meet his, afraid of what she might see.

There was no regret or anger. He was looking at her as if counting the ways he might devour her. His interest was clear, and it was a notch or two above the friendly neighbor variety. She may as well be lying in the sun for the intensity she felt on her skin.

Suddenly smug and satisfied, Eve perched on the edge of the couch with the intent of bringing them back to a more stable topic of conversation but was interrupted by the doorbell. She swung disappointed eyes to the door and saw her brother through the stained glass inset.

Frustration bubbled in her gut and was echoed in a single word when Trey grudgingly pulled his hands back out of his pockets and growled, "Hell."

~~~

How was it that someone or something always interrupted his time with Eve? Trey silently complained about the timing as he watched her unfold those long legs and stride back to the foyer. He noted the furrow of concern between her brows as she stepped back to let Lance, who had already let himself in, pass by with Gabrielle on his heels. Neither of them was calm, and Trey knew this was no simple visit.

Her brother caught Trey's eye and must have realized his transparency as he pasted on a smile and cut Eve off before she could begin an inquisition. "Hey, it's biting outside. Got any hot chocolate handy?"

Eve tapped one foot on the floor and gave both visitors a lingering look but headed to the kitchen. "I'll have to nuke the water. No stove." The clip of her words conveyed displeasure with whatever situation Lance and Gabrielle were about to share.

Trey sized up the tall Viking of a man. His asking for hot chocolate was comical.

Lance must have felt the scrutiny, since he nodded at him. "Trey Rainwater, isn't it? Nan mentioned you."

Unsure how much Nan had actually revealed to her grandson, Trey kept his response generic. "She mentioned you, too." He acknowledged Gabrielle then returned his attention to Lance. "I have a feeling we're meeting under less than ideal conditions."

Eve's brother frowned. "Look, I hate to be rude..."

"Then don't," Eve called from the kitchen, amidst the sound of clinking glassware. "Anyone else want a drink?"

Lance and Gabrielle shared a mutual moment of silence before Lance tossed his hand in a gesture that invited Trey to follow. "I guess you're in."

Trey briefly considered leaving and allowing them some privacy, but an even stronger inclination guided his feet toward the back of the house. To Eve.

Her head was bent forward while she examined the pages of a magazine. The feigned interest in the colorful pages indicated her upset. Trey clenched and opened his fists, already wishing he could take out his frustration on whatever or whoever caused her stress.

He'd finally seen her relax, enough to let her know he wanted her. Now she was nervous again and doing her best to downplay it. Trouble seemed to follow Eve like a stray dog.

Surprisingly, Gabrielle was the first to speak, and she was obviously of the pull-the-band-aid-off-fast variety. "It's about the girl they thought went missing at Taylor-Grant." She shot the words out like she might change her mind if given the chance.

"The college in Verde Hill?" Eve stopped flipping through the magazine and focused on her brother's worried face then back to her friend. "I haven't heard anything about it. What do you mean they thought she was missing?"

Gabrielle casually moved to stand beside Eve, but the tightness of her posture told Trey the woman despised talking about the dreadful issue. "I didn't mention it, but I knew they thought foul play might have been a factor."

Huffing out a breath, Gabrielle continued. "You know the spiel. Wait twenty-four hours before filing a missing person's report. Did she run off with some guy or just decide to ditch her life? A trip to California that she neglected to mention. To anyone."

Comprehension was apparent as Eve's face faded into a paler version of itself. Her brother and Gabrielle showing up together. The looks on their faces as if about to deliver bad news, or expecting to get some. Trey could practically feel her tremble.

Her eyes searched out Trey's. He had remained silent since the arrival of the others, but he suddenly wanted to walk them back out the door and save Eve from what they were determined to tell her.

Eve squared her shoulders and addressed Gabrielle and Lance. "Why are you both speaking in the past tense? She's no longer missing, is that it?"

"They're looking at college kids and her boyfriend." Gabrielle rushed her words in an attempt to placate Eve. "Kids today can really get themselves into trouble."

Lance delivered the blow. "They found her body this morning, Eve. It hasn't hit the papers yet, but Todd called me.

He thought I... that we should know."

Lips pressed into a thin, painful line, Eve nodded. Her arms wrapped around her waist as if attempting to hold something in. The recovery of any dead body was unpleasant, but he imagined violence of one human to another was especially hard for Eve.

"They think it was isolated? Someone she knew?" Eve plunged ahead, her expression hopeful for anything that might be taken as encouragement. That would make this an everyday tragedy, if there were such a thing.

Gabrielle was quick to respond. "That's what they think."

"They're still investigating." Lance steeled his jaw to back up his opinion, but wasn't quite able to distract Eve from the pause that had preceded his response. It had been a split-second too long.

She took a step away from her brother, but forged ahead with her questioning. "There's more. Tell me what you know, Lance. I'm sure Todd wanted you to know for a reason. He wanted you to prepare me. For what?"

Her brother raked a hand through his hair, his features tight with distress. "The body. What was done to her..."

He didn't finish, but Trey wouldn't have been paying any more attention if he had. His focus was now on Eve. She had doubled over, her eyes rounding as she looked into empty air. A low, heartrending sound seeped from her throat then formed into words. One word.

"No," she moaned, clasping her hands over her eyes as she crumpled to the floor.

Gabrielle was closest and lunged in to ease her friend down to the ground with care.

Trey started to go to them but was blocked by Lance. "You should go. Now."

"What's happening?" Trey asked, trying to maneuver around him.

"Please." Eve's brother gripped his upper arms fiercely, but his eyes pleaded. "She wouldn't want you to see this."

Trey wanted to go to Eve, but was once again the outsider no one was sure could be trusted. Despite his background and all his training, he didn't know what to do. He didn't understand what the hell was happening.

Eve's brother threw a fearful glance to where the two women sat huddled together, Gabrielle stroking Eve's back. Maybe Lance was right. They could take care of it.

Respecting the man's wishes and what he believed Eve would want as well, Trey said nothing more, but slipped away like a spirit, leaving them in peace.

But knowing he would be back.

Seven

"What is this exactly?" Gabrielle held the box away from her body as if it offended her sensibilities. A silver object, rectangular and set at a tilt, was pictured on the outside.

"It's a mandoline," Eve educated her friend, taking the box from her. "Exactly what I've been looking for."

"Isn't that a musical instrument?"

Eve rolled her eyes. She was never at a loss for entertainment with Gabrielle. "No, that's a mandolin, which I'm sure you very well know." She rubbed a loving hand along the package before setting it in her cart. "It's stainless steel and will be invaluable for appetizer trays."

Gabrielle leaned over and read from the label, "Easily produces perfect julienne, matchstick, French fry, and crinkle cuts on any vegetable." She fluttered eyelashes at Eve and placed a hand over her heart. "Why Eve, you'll simply be all the rage."

"Tell me again why I brought you shopping?" Eve asked with a wry, lopsided grin.

"Because I left my store in Joni's capable twenty-something hands, so I could spend the day helping my best friend look for implements the Marquis de Sade would envy."

Taking in the gleam of the display items and their blades, Eve nodded. "He could be very creative with these."

Both women stopped and simultaneously scrunched up their noses at the distasteful pictures popping to mind.

"Right. On to the paper doilies, please." Gabrielle lifted the heavy mass of loose curls off her neck and tossed them down the back of her red velvet jacket.

Eyeing the bright fabric, Eve stated, "After we're done here, you can take me to wherever you buy your clothes."

Gabrielle twirled back with a maniacal gleam in her eyes. "Promise? Oh, I've been dying to get my hands on your wardrobe for years."

"Watch it or I'll be forced to tell you all about..." Eve's voice trailed off when she spied an open box lined with black satin and filled with a multitude of silver cutting devices with wooden handles. "Chinese garnishing tools." She sighed.

"No, please. Anything but that." Gabrielle was teasing again, but she obviously knew mouthwatering when she saw it, and Eve was positively entranced. "So buy it," she said.

Eve shook her head. "Nope. I can't justify it."

"Well, I can." Gabrielle snatched one of the sets and put it in the cart. "Welcome home present. Now I don't have to worry if I got you something you'll like."

With a squeal that only women understood, Eve danced in place and hugged her friend. "Thank you, thank you, thank you." She pulled back. "That's the third homecoming gift I've gotten. Maybe I should have a party and really rake it in."

They continued their browsing through the aisles of the chef supply store, Eve stocking up on essentials that would serve for any occasion, cutlery, mixing bowls, serving platters. She was fairly well stocked already, since cooking was her joy, but needed items for producing large quantities.

Inspecting a set of service plates with leopard print edging, Gabrielle sighed and asked, "So who were the other presents from?"

"Huh? Oh, a plant from Lance and a...this is going to sound weird, but Trey is sort of helping me get a van." Eve felt her cheeks pinken and was mortified. The result of her inner response to Trey did not go unnoticed.

"Well, well. A van. Guess he's not the wine and roses

type." Gabrielle went back to perusing the odd assortment of glassware.

"Oh, I think he's that, too." She saw her friend's arched eyebrow and raised one of her own in response. "Not that we're going there. At least, not yet."

"Did he actually buy you a car?"

"No, he just found me a good deal and is going to fix it up. In return, I'll cater when he needs it." Eve stood her ground against Gabrielle's dubious expression. "What's going on inside that Gypsy brain of yours?"

Gabrielle dropped the napkins she had been holding and sighed again. "I don't know. I'm getting a bad vibe."

Eve knew all about Gabrielle's vibes and that they were based on truth more often than not. "About Trey?" Eve didn't want that to be the case. For once she hoped her friend was wrong.

"I'm not sure. It feels like some negative presence is closer to you than when you first came back, and the only new person in your life is Trey, right?" Gabrielle puckered her lips in remorse. "I'm sorry. I hope I'm off. Way off. Because you seem different when you talk about him, but I'd be a bad friend if I didn't tell you."

"You know you can say anything to me." Eve smiled. "We'll just have to see how things go. I can tell you, I do have some misgivings about Trey, but whenever he leaves..." Eve shook her head. "All I want is to see him again."

Frowning, Gabrielle asked, "Speaking of which, have you talked to him since yesterday?"

Eve didn't want to remember the scene at her house and the complete loss of control she'd experienced. In front of Trey. "No. I've been trying to think of what to tell him. I can blame it on over-reaction, and he would believe it had something to do with my past. He read the article, so he knows enough to put two and two together. I just don't want him to think I'm..." She trailed off, unable to vocalize the embarrassment that had always followed whenever anyone found out about her "attacks."

"You don't want him to think you're crazy?" Gabrielle didn't mince words.

"You remember what happened with Robert. He was with me when I saw something, for lack of a better explanation, and he called it off the next day." Eve shuddered. The only chink in her armor was what people would say if they knew she was not only haunted by memories but disabled at times. She didn't want to be seen as a freak.

"He was a jerk, and you're better off. Do you trust Trey?" Gabrielle probed.

"In some ways, absolutely, but in other areas, I think he's a bad bet."

"What ways?"

Eve stopped and leaned onto the handle of the shopping buggy. "He's inherently a good man. I'm sure he is, but he gives off this constant I'm-a-loner-slash-nomad aura. I remind myself daily to keep my guard up where he's concerned."

"Hmm." Gabrielle opened her little black purse and popped a ball of gum into her mouth. "How about having some unattached sex? You could use all the endorphins at your disposal with the stress you're going through. First losing Nan, now the house and a new business." She chewed the gum thoughtfully. "Yes, definitely calls for some intra-sheet calisthenics."

Tilting her head in agreement, Eve said, "Oh, I have no trouble envisioning that. It's just that, I like him. I enjoy talking to him. I even enjoy not talking to him."

"I enjoy not talking to most men." Gabrielle grinned at her own humor.

"You know what I mean, a companionable silence. I feel like we could just sit and have coffee together, me working on a recipe, him doing whatever a computer jock does." The more she thought about it, Eve was absolutely disgruntled. She put her hands on her hips. "Damn. I think I've got a crush."

Gabrielle couldn't hide her amusement. "Honey, you don't have a crush. You've got a glow, and that's a much more serious condition."

"But I barely know him," Eve protested.

Gabrielle glanced over at her slack-jawed friend. "I know, and there's your trouble." She patted Eve on the shoulder then offered her a piece of gum and some Gypsy-style comfort. "Don't worry. I'll light a candle."

~~~

Sturg's Diner boasted the best open-faced, hot sandwiches in Georgia and offered a pleasing 1950's Doo-Wop setting to go along with it. The floors were a checkered pattern of white and aqua-blue, counters were trimmed in a shiny chrome-like material, and the red stools at the bar picked up the bright color in various vintage pictures lining the walls.

Eve particularly liked one of a young red-headed girl delivering milkshakes on roller skates. It was an escape into simpler times, and she was grateful Gabrielle had suggested it.

"That's the owner, Sturg, back in the kitchen," Gabrielle pointed out. "He takes great pride in both the diner and his cooking abilities. You two should have plenty to talk about."

Eve glimpsed a portion of the man's left cheek but the rest of his face was hidden behind a wheel of hanging tickets. He really did do things the old way. Even the cash register made a *ca-ching* as opposed to the silence of a modern computer-operated version.

Eve didn't remember much about him, as was the case with many people from Pine Creek, even if they were her age. After the "incident," Eve had been home-schooled until graduating early at the age of seventeen. Then she couldn't get out of town fast enough.

The only close friend she had retained through the years was Gabrielle. The two of them had known each other since second grade when Gabrielle had called Eve's legs "scrawny chicken cast-offs," and Eve had responded by punching her in the lip.

They'd been bread and butter ever since.

When the waitress arrived to take their orders, Eve opted for a French dip combo while Gabrielle asked for a fried chicken salad but requested so many substitutions it turned into a whole new creation. "Okay," the young blonde said with some hesitation before leaving the two of them alone again.

"Back to what I mentioned earlier," Gabrielle said, "You should wear the black shirt."

Eve sipped her diet soda and laughed out a breath before responding. "You've mentioned a few things today, and I need somewhere to go to wear that."

"You do have somewhere to go. Next door."

Eve hooted. "And he would know exactly what I had in mind when he opened the door. Might as well carry a red lantern over with me."

"That's where you have your opportunity to throw him a few curveballs. Tit for tat." Gabrielle's grin was devious at best and would have sent fear racing down the spine of any common sense male had they been there to witness it. "Offer a little temptation, but let him know you're not to be trifled with. The man's got you boggled, so you need to hit back with your full arsenal."

"You make it sound like war."

Gabrielle steeled her smile. "Has love ever been anything else?"

Trying to veer away from the idea of love and war, Eve asked, "So why the black?"

"You've got great curves that don't have to be flaunted to be appreciated. The square neckline shows off your collar bones."

"Collar bones? I thought I was going for sexy?"

Gabrielle made a disgusted sound. "Trust me on this one." She dumped another packet of sweetener into her tea. "And you need to wear your hair back."

Eve crossed her arms and asked the question with her eyes.

"Neck and cheekbones," Gabrielle answered.

"The women I see on television must have a different version of what attracts a man," Eve countered, still unconvinced.

"That depends on the kind of man you're after, and something tells me Trey Rainwater looks deeper."

"Something tells me that, too, and it doesn't make me feel any better." Eve reflected on her words. It was the depth she sensed beneath Trey's surface that aroused her and threw aside any inhibitions. He was honest about his wandering ways, but Eve believed there was more to him. She knew he was the leaving kind, but somehow she felt he would be there to protect her. It was up to her to protect herself from Trey.

A heavy ceramic bowl slammed on the table, jarring Eve and Gabrielle. Eve looked up to see a man who vaguely resembled a bulldog towering over them. He glared at her then slid her sandwich onto the apple red Formica as well.

Eve tensed as waves of animosity rolled off of him. She took note of his clenched fists and shifted into defense mode.

Gabrielle was calm, but her eyes and tone of voice would have chilled an iceberg. "Is there a problem, Sturg?"

He cast an annoyed look to her but quickly returned his scrutiny to Eve. What was wrong with him? Chemical imbalance? Eve didn't even know him, but he was treating her like she'd brought the plague into his restaurant instead of patronage.

"Seems to me like you two are the ones with the problem. If you don't like the way I make things then don't come in." He folded thick arms across his chest and curled his upper lip to drive home the point.

"You must be mistaken, because we haven't made any complaints," Eve said through clenched teeth. She didn't appreciate being accosted for no good reason.

"You come in here and change around my salad like you know better," he said to Gabrielle. "And don't think I don't know who told you to." He ground out the last remark then proceeded to lean down toward Eve. "We don't need no fancy caterers coming in here and tellin' us how to do things. In fact, we don't need no caterers at all. I handle the needs here."

Eve had a comment on the tip of her tongue about paranoia and how psych medicines were getting better every day, but Gabrielle fired back with one of her own. And she nailed the raging bull's weak spot.

"Come on, Sturg. I don't think hot dogs and potato chips qualify as cuisine." She lifted innocent eyes and offered a weak smile, but her words dripped with venom. "Eve doesn't have any plans to compete with you in that area, so don't worry about battling for customers. I assure you, there won't be any competition."

Eve summoned a smile she hoped might pass as sincere, though her face felt starched. "Why would I come here, if I viewed you as a rival? Honestly, the thought never entered my mind. Gabrielle said this was a great place to eat, so here we are."

"And you know how I have to have things my way, Sturg." Gabrielle winked at him, and his features twisted into a mix of anger and confusion. He probably didn't know what to make of the two females and their prettily, but barely, sheathed claws.

"Whatever. I better not hear of you two bad-mouthing me or my place." Before he left, Sturg poked his finger at Eve. "Don't think I don't know all about you."

He stalked away but left a wake of cold ripples that found their way into Eve's belly. She felt nauseated by his parting shot and met Gabrielle's shocked and furious eyes. "Let's just go. We can get lunch somewhere else."

"No way. I'm going to drag him back over here to apologize. That was way out of line." She clasped Eve's hand. "I'm so sorry. I've never seen him act so crazy." She lifted one corner of her mouth. "Your reputation must precede you, and I'm talking about your culinary skills, not the other thing. He's probably afraid you'll put him out of business."

Eve shook her head. "That's just ridiculous beyond belief. He owns a restaurant." Eve held up open palms as if they were a set of scales and moved them as she spoke. "Apples and kumquats. No comparison."

"None." Gabrielle looked at their plates. "I'm hungry, and I don't like giving in to bullies."

"Me, either. I'm already planning what I'll order for dessert." Eve cut into her food with relish.

"Speaking of dessert, I was going to save my surprise until coffee and cake time but think you could use some good news now." Gabrielle took a bite of salad, purposefully dragging out the suspense while Eve waited expectantly.

"I have a job for you." She sat forward, excitement lighting her up. "It's a wedding!"

Swallowing hard to clear her throat, Eve gushed, "You're joking. I haven't even picked my name out yet. I was going to get your opinion on that." Thrilled with the news, Eve started to babble. "I'm so excited. A wedding reception is the perfect way to get good references and a lot at once."

"That was the good news," Gabrielle said before adding, "The bad news is the wedding's pretty soon. The mother of the groom was going to do it herself until the bride had a meltdown over the menu. Her sister is a frequent customer of mine and told me the whole story, and I, um, sort of volunteered you."

"How soon is soon?"

"October seventeenth." Gabrielle sat back and scrunched her face as if waiting for a blow.

"That's next Saturday." Eve mentally tallied the days. "I would literally have seven days. Eight if I start today, and I haven't met with them or figured out a budget."

"But you said it would be great promotion, and I'll help. We'll get it done. Joni used to be a server, and she said she would do it and also has a friend who serves."

Pushing her plate aside, Eve opened her purse and pulled

out a day-planner. An orange envelope fell out of the pages. "Oh, here. Before I forget, I think you dropped this at my house the other day." She handed Gabrielle the poem.

Her friend perused the words but shook her head. "This isn't mine. I've never seen it."

"It must have been dropped off at the wrong house, because it makes no sense to me." Still harried about the possibility of planning a large event on such short notice, Eve stuck the note in the back of her book and started making a list of things she would need for the wedding.

After a few minutes of scribbling, she looked back up at Gabrielle. "I'll need to speak with the bride right away, but I think I can do it."

"I know you can. It will be perfect, and you'll be established more quickly than you would have been with a month's worth of advertising." Gabrielle waved to their waitress. "Okay, coffee and chocolate to re-energize, then we have to get to work." She produced a small black phone. "I'll call Elle. She's the blushing bride."

Blowing out a breath for calm, Eve gave a slow nod of acquiescence before accepting the phone and entering into conversation with a very chatty young bride. When she hung up, she had a clear image of what she was in for.

"So what now?" Gabrielle asked.

"I have to hit the drawing board and start planning the menu, get her approval and deposit, then go back to the supply store once the courses are finalized. She already has someone for the cake, and I already have the business license working." Eve smiled broadly. "I can't believe it's finally happening."

Their chocolate lava cake and raspberry cheesecake arrived, prompting both women to dive in. "You working on the menu tonight?" Gabrielle asked as she licked a finger.

"Maybe a little," Eve said with a devilish smile. "But first, I have to see a man about a van."

EIGHT

Trey sat back in the black leather office chair and rubbed his face. He'd been working on the computer for two hours and needed a break. Creating the unique language or "code" that would produce an actual image on the Internet was something he never got tired of, but his eyes did.

It was a good thing dinner would be arriving soon, and he couldn't imagine a more desirable form of delivery than the one he'd been offered.

The doorbell chimed low, sonorous notes. She was here.

He opened the door to see Eve with a large picnic basket in her arms and bags hanging from her elbows. He leaned in to take some of the burden and caught her scent. It reminded him of gardenias and pumpkin pie, creating an amendment to his earlier thought. He could imagine something more desirable.

"Let me get those," he offered, looking at the plastic bags.

Eve stepped past him. "That's okay. They aren't as heavy as the basket. I'll just put them in the kitchen?" she asked and paused.

"You don't have to ask. I won't turn down food." Trey set the basket on the counter and flipped on more lighting. Pale green tiles of glass lined the lower portion of the kitchen walls and were the only source of color in the room other than a metal basket filled with fruit.

Eve nodded her approval. "Minimalist. I like it."

"But not your style?"

She shrugged. "Parts of it."

Removing various food items and plastic containers, she emptied the bags then removed heavier dishes from the basket.

He watched Eve as she worked, dressed in faded jeans and a black top that clung to her curves. The dark shirt covered her arms to the elbows while leaving a little more skin exposed at the neckline.

His eyes followed the edges of the fabric along sun-kissed skin then up to her face, appreciating the classic bone structure emphasized by her hairstyle. The thick gold that normally hung past her shoulders was twisted into an intricate braid and small blue stones dangled at her ears. Despite the jeans, she seemed regal. A Viking princess was standing beside his toaster.

Trey decided he could use a drink. "I was surprised when you called," he said, walking to the refrigerator. "Would you like some wine or beer?"

"White, if you have it." She was placing something in the sink. "Do you have a colander?"

Trey set down the wine and bottle of beer he'd removed and moved to stand beside her before reaching above to a cabinet. His chest pressed into her for a moment, and the rush from the slight touch was unsettling.

Dropping the metal colander into the sink, he swiftly went back to his beer and opened the Pinot Grigio for Eve. *I can't believe I just got turned on by a shoulder.*

He opted to focus on another basic human need. "What are we having?" he asked.

"Braised lamb shanks with trumpet royale mushrooms and zinfandel," she replied without batting an eye as she lifted a large covered pot out of the basket. Placing it near the oven, she set the appliance to her desired temperature and went back to work.

"Which brings me back to my question. What did I do to deserve a gourmet meal?" He watched her narrow waist and the taut muscles of her back move beneath her shirt while she sliced mushrooms.

"I wanted to thank you again for offering what you did with the car, and this is the best way for me to do that." She stopped and twisted to meet his eyes. "I also needed to sweeten the pot, so to speak, since I need to amp up the favor a little."

"How so?"

Dropping the knife onto the wooden cutting board she had confiscated from its hiding place, Eve turned to face him fully. "Is there any way the van could be usable by Saturday? Not perfect, just passable. I have a job offer. A wedding, which is the golden egg in this business."

Trey could tell it was torquing her pride to have to ask. "We were aiming for Sunday, actually, so we can get it done with a few more hours."

"I'll pay extra."

He held up a hand. "We've already been through that. If I feel you owe me something I'll let you know."

The sound of fungi being sliced resumed. "You said 'we.' Who else is working with you?"

"My friend Sam. We met at a sporting goods store and realized we had the love of grease in common as well as fishing. The van's at his place, actually. His garage is better outfitted."

"He doesn't mind?"

"No, but I'm cutting him in. Don't worry."

The expression she made told him he'd hit on exactly what she was thinking.

"Can I help you with anything?" He decided to risk standing close to her again, and swore to himself he would have more control than the day before at her house. He hadn't planned on kissing her. In fact, he still felt any involvement with her was a major conflict of interest.

She had no idea he'd agreed to keep an eye on her long before her return to Pine Creek. Living next door, he was in the position to ensure she actually resided in her grandmother's house for the required year and didn't slip out of town when the lawyer wasn't looking. He hadn't taken any money, though it had been offered. He was simply honoring the request of a friend.

It was his sense of honor that had guilt slipping onto the back of his conscience every time he thought of getting closer to Eve. There was the small matter of his deceit in not telling her the whole truth. That was bad enough. Moving in on the granddaughter Nan had trusted him to look out for... that was the dirty bomb just waiting to blow his principles all to hell.

He tried to justify his actions, telling himself that being friends with Eve would keep her close, enabling him to assure Kurt Dennis of her whereabouts. There was no harm in that. He again appreciated the long lines of her physique and held his breath. Taking her to bed, well, that might cross a few lines.

"Would you hand me the oils in the basket?"

Eve's words did nothing to guide Trey's imaginings back to the straight and narrow. He wondered what type of oils she meant and briefly imagined a sensual glimmer on her skin. Damning his own thoughts, he instead looked in and located two glass vials. "What kind of oils are these?" He hoped his voice sounded normal again, because every movement felt restrained and tense.

"Grape seed and peanut." She washed her hands and transferred the mushrooms to a bowl. "I also need a large frying pan. Sorry to make a mess, but I couldn't lug everything I needed over. The Dutch oven was all I could manage, and I assumed you might not have one."

"You assumed correctly. I don't know what a Dutch oven is and never knew you could get oil from a grape seed." He was at a disadvantage in more ways than one tonight, something he was not accustomed to.

While Eve sautéed the ingredients in the pan he'd provided and browned the lamb, Trey found himself more interested in cooking than he'd ever been in his life. MREs had always served well enough on missions, as did his microwave skills when home, but Eve's knowledge and confidence in the kitchen was fascinating. She moved with coordination and timing, juggling tomatoes, wine, and seasonings as if performing a well-rehearsed dance.

"You love what you do," he said with a sudden realization of how good she really was.

She laughed without taking her eyes off of her handiwork. "I do, and I learned from another like me."

"Nan?"

"Uh-huh. She was a natural, more than I ever was, but I have the secret weapon of exposure to a variety of cooking styles. I've traveled and studied a little, mixing what I saw abroad with my own tricks." She slid the Dutch oven into his oven, which he decided not to question, then slapped her hands together in a manner that told him she was done.

"That's going to take a while, so I also have some appetizers," she told him and pulled plastic wrap from a plate.

Trey sampled the as yet unidentified dip she offered by smearing some on one of the oversized crackers surrounding it. He made a sound of intense pleasure. "If dinner comes close to this, then you're even better than I thought."

Eve smiled triumphantly and with a hint of something wicked in her eye. "I'm not going to touch that one."

He took another bite. "The old saying about the way to a man's heart never worried me before, but I think you may have put something extra in this." Cocking a playful eyebrow, he smiled. "Any magic spells I should be aware of?"

Eve laughed. "No. That would be Gabrielle's department, but even she believes it's all psychological." She stepped closer. "Me, I'm a chemist. The right combination of natural elements and even an always-in-control guy like yourself would beg for mercy."

"Are we talking about food or sex?" Trey tried not to notice her pink lips or the brief flicker of her tongue as she moistened them.

"Both. Many cultures consider certain foods to be aphrodisiacs."

"Right. Oysters and bologna." Trey pondered a moment. "I don't see it."

Eve tried one of the treats herself and sighed. "You're right. I am good." After sipping her wine, she added, "I've never heard about bologna, but besides oysters, you have bananas, ginseng, truffles, and of course the obvious ones like champagne and chocolate. Oh, and figs."

"New meaning behind the whole fig leaf as clothing theory." Trey loosened a collar that was already loose. "I'll never look at fruit the same way again."

Obviously enjoying herself, Eve leaned against the counter. "It's not all about the physical. Love went hand in hand. If someone prepared you a meal of lobster and asparagus, it might have been the equivalent of today's red roses. The Egyptians, in fact, favored radishes."

"Any of that in this dip?"

The implication of Trey's question registered, and he saw Eve's light blue eyes darken as her mouth parted slightly. She drew a ragged breath and touched her hair, timeless body language. She probably didn't realize what she was telling him.

Recognizing the need for retreat, Trey took her wine glass and refilled it before grabbing another beer from the fridge. "Come with me. There's something I want to show you."

As expected, she followed him to his parlor, now serving as office, where he pulled up an extra seat in front of the computer. He sat and motioned for her to take his more comfortable executive chair.

Eyeing the electronics, dual monitors, and paperwork, Eve said, "I don't want to spill my drink."

She set it on a bookshelf and returned to sit beside him. Her leg knocked against his, and Trey found himself trying to refocus again.

Sliding the mouse on a plain black pad, he roused the screen from its sleep and clicked on an icon named "Eve." An elegant website with ivory, beige, and sage as the color theme opened.

Eve gasped then read over the basic information before asking Trey to hit the tab that read "menu."

A drop-down appeared with small, empty boxes. "You can fill these with basics, like entrees and appetizers or another option, that I would recommend is listing general types of menus such as wedding, corporate express, themed, small plates. Whatever you planned on branching into."

She nodded, engrossed in the images. "What's the 'Plan Your Party' tab?"

Trey moved the pointer and another list appeared, but this time there were options.

"Event checklist, event sites, partner vendors," Eve read aloud. "I love this, but I can tell it will be a lot more work."

"You can add basic information as you go or I can remove anything you don't feel is appropriate." For the first time in his career, Trey was nervous showing a client the first draft of a website. "You can change styles and colors. I wanted to work up a basic site as a starting point. Show you some options."

"This is amazing. It's exactly my style. Even the colors." She placed a hand on his and met his eyes. "Thank you. I had imagined a really plain and serviceable website. I guess that's why I'm a cook and you're a site designer."

Trey enjoyed the warmth of her touch and wrapped her fingers in his, bringing their joined hands to rest on his thigh. "This is what comes naturally to me. Like working on cars. I can envision the end product, but get a bigger thrill from the mechanics that go into making it happen."

"Show me yours."

Trey wasn't sure what she meant.

"You have a website for your company, right?" Eve said when he didn't catch on.

After an understanding grunt, Trey typed an address and a black screen with metallic trim opened. A wave of what looked like quicksilver slid across the top.

"Nice," Eve whispered with true appreciation. "That's definitely you." She skimmed the page's contents. "Rainwater Site Design." She looked again at Trey with a hint of wonder. "Quite an accomplishment, your company. It must have taken more than a little commitment and work."

He wasn't one to brag, but he didn't put much stock in false modesty either. "It did. Three offices now. The others are in San Francisco and Phoenix."

"Pine Creek doesn't really fit in. Why did you choose a smaller city for this one?"

Trey couldn't honestly answer, since he wasn't sure himself. "Like I told you the day we met, my parents are closer, and I might have imagined small town life as something I would enjoy. It was a change, and somewhere I've never been is usually the only place I want to be."

"You did tell me you were a wanderer, didn't you? Never one to stay in one place too long." Eve seemed to suddenly find the keyboard very interesting and lightly ran her fingertips over the letters. "Do you still plan to leave once you've had enough of what Pine Creek has to offer?"

Trey didn't like where this was leading, but he didn't want to lie to her any more than he had to. "Probably. It's who I am."

Eve slid her hand away. "I need to check on dinner."

She stood and smiled, but it lacked the warmth and promise from earlier. Trey missed both.

He stayed where he was but heard her words float back as she walked away. "I really like the website. Let's keep the design the way it is."

Remaining silent, he broke the Internet connection and rose to join Eve in the other room. He noticed her forgotten wine glass on the book shelf.

There was no mistaking the change in their moods. Eve had thrown up an invisible wall, and Trey found himself oddly taken aback. He wanted to be honest with her, whatever that meant after everything he'd gotten involved in. Lawyers, spying, promises.

And why did any of it matter? He would be leaving when the time came, because permanent was something he didn't do. Relationships were something he didn't want. He was a nomad. Always on the lookout for the next challenge.

Eve was obviously interested in more than he had to offer, or she wouldn't be trying so hard to protect herself. A brief fling was not on her agenda, and regrettably, he found that even more appealing. No matter how much he wanted Eve, he respected her, and in more ways than he'd imagined.

He headed toward the aroma of baking lamb and the delicious woman who would be sharing it with him. He would be a gentleman, he would take pleasure in Eve's company tonight, and he would let her walk out the door when it was over.

And remind himself he owed her that.

~~~

Having left the cookware with Trey, after promises he would wash and return them the next day, Eve's load was considerably lighter for the walk home. Her heart was heavier.

Every time I think we've connected, he reminds me it's an impossibility. Why do I keep setting myself up for failure? Eve trudged through the leaves, unimpressed by the beauty of the fall night and its midnight blue sky.

She felt like a fool, after all her talk of aphrodisiacs and the use of food to convey emotion. "Mr. ex-Marine just up and said, 'Nope. Sorry. I'm outta' here.' " Eve realized her voice might have carried on the wind and glanced back to make sure she was alone.

No sign of Trey. He was probably watching her from his window to make sure she got in all right, so she faced forward again, hoping he hadn't seen her look back. "I wouldn't doubt it if he had on night vision goggles," she said in a more subdued tone. "Wouldn't want him to have to get too close."

As she turned the key, she reluctantly admitted she was as angry with herself as she was with him, for thinking his kiss had meant something. She was more humiliated now than when she'd broken down in front of him. She'd hoped to put her meltdown behind her and almost had with the excitement of planning for the wedding gig. Now it washed over her again like a cold bucket of water, and she felt like a lovesick pre-teen.

Locking the door behind her, Eve turned to go up the stairs when a flash of color caught her eye. She looked straight down the hallway and through the kitchen to the window over her new farmhouse sink. Her eyes zeroed in on the orange square.

Trying to rationalize what she saw, she moved toward the glass and the envelope hanging there. It was taped to the window, where it wouldn't be missed.

Eve dreaded going outside again to get it. The atmosphere seemed more threatening and the night filled with more shadows. She already knew what was inside but didn't understand why someone was leaving them here.

Her lungs helplessly worked to pull in air as she froze with the sudden surety that this poem, and therefore the last, were both meant for her. A gust of wind tossed up the envelope then slapped it back against the clear glass, making sure she got the message.

There was no doubt this time. The truth was spelled out clearly across the paper, in three jagged, angry letters.

That spelled her name.

NINE

This one had been a rush job. Not nearly as much fun as stalking the student.

He wasn't ashamed to use the word stalk, because that's what he did. He hunted his prey, learned their patterns, and knew their weaknesses.

The student had been too wrapped up in her own petty problems to recognize real trouble until it walked up and shoved a cloth over her face.

His latest victim was too vain. So sure of his ability to talk, or if that failed, buy his way out a sticky situation, that he never questioned the wisdom of going with a stranger to the middle of nowhere to share some pot. Now look where that had gotten him.

The male wouldn't be as much fun as the girls, that went without saying, but he fit the pattern and would have to do.

The poor guy's eyes were bulging in terror, and his nose leaked from crying, something the man who held him captive found disgusting. "Calm down. This won't take long." The killer spit tobacco into a stained plastic trash can sitting beside his work bench. An array of tools were laid out in no particular order.

The table was gouged and stained, having been used often over the years. Anything that was worth doing was worth doing well, and perfection required practice. The killer had learned that over the years.

He considered the gun, for its ability to get the job done

quickly, but decided the noise and mess weren't worth the trade-off. He could cut the guy's throat, but would have to go to the trouble of positioning him over the drain, and spreading a tarp in case his victim managed to struggle too much. Not that either.

Nothing seemed right.

Damn it. Why did it have to be a man? I'm not feeling this.

But it had to be done. He knew this as surely as he knew he would meet his own end one day. He could hear the words now, being whispered calmly. Persistently.

There's no getting out of this. It must be done, and you are the one that must do it. It must be done. It must be done.

A wet snort behind him made the killer cringe. Blood he was used to, but the sound of all that mucous was making him sick.

"You need to stop crying," he told his captive with the serenity of a priest addressing a forlorn parishioner. "I'm not going to un-tape your mouth, and if your nose stops up, you could suffocate."

He stared at the man's nostrils as they flared and ran with snot. He seemed to be working pretty hard at it already. "Now why didn't I think of that?"

Passing the tool-covered table he stepped into a cramped closet and retrieved a heavy-duty black garbage bag. He would be done in no time and still able to catch the game later. Maybe he'd pick up some Chinese food.

The killer returned to the restrained man and spoke again in a soothing voice. "I'm sorry, this really isn't your fault, but due to circumstances beyond my control, it's something I must do." He whipped the bag twice to open it. "And in all honestly, I may have lied before. I don't know how long this will take."

~~~

"No, they weren't overtly threatening, but that doesn't change the fact someone has been sneaking around my house." Eve kicked at the base of the staircase, imagining herself ripping off the floral runner that covered the wood and refinishing the natural treasure that lay beneath. Maybe that would ease her frustration. The cop, a woman who sounded gruff and stout, was unimpressed by Eve's report of strange poems. She kept referring to them as love notes.

"They aren't from anyone I know or would care to know," Eve continued to argue. The policewoman told her there was little they could do without further proof, but Eve should call nine-one-one if anyone trespassed while she was home.

After the line had disconnected, Eve said to no one, "Thanks. You've been a great help."

She went about the business of gathering her notes and the employment application Gabrielle had given her. The form was straightforward, but Eve had a few questions of her own she wanted to ask the boy coming for an interview. He'd been a referral of Joni's, the girl who worked for Gabrielle. A friend of a friend. That's how it was in college, barely-there relationships with a hundred people you would probably never speak to again after graduation.

Hitting the power button on the coffee maker, Eve reflected on her own cynicism. *Not everyone is as anti-social as I am. Or Trey.*

Realizing she'd just attributed herself with the same trait she disliked in Trey, Eve wondered if she was being unfair. She was fiercely protective of her privacy and the dark secret that clung to her adult life, even though the incident had occurred in her childhood and she'd suffered through the appropriate amount of therapy.

Trey, in quite the same manner, was protective of his...his what exactly? His freedom? That seemed to sum it up best. He wanted new places, new challenges, and evidently, to Eve's displeasure, new faces. But he'd been honest and had never altered his story. How could she blame him for that?

"And why do I care enough to be upset? Why can't I just do

what Gabrielle suggested and take what he offers then move on?" Eve asked herself the questions as she slammed an empty cup down on the counter. The action was followed by a wince before she ran her hand over the new espresso granite to check for damage and thankfully found none.

She had to get a handle on this thing with Trey.

Gabrielle wasn't the only one who could sense things, though Eve would never go head-to-head with her in that arena. Eve confronted her own reasons for letting Trey's attitude upset her. She tossed her head back, closed her eyes, and envisioned the moment at his computer when he'd told her again that he would leave. His deep brown eyes flashed before her, and she knew.

"Because I don't believe him," she said in awe. There had been a well-concealed but still evident emotion behind Trey's words that night. For a man trying so hard to keep her at arm's length, he had looked miserable. Not worried or concerned, over her hurt feelings or his wings being clipped, but dejected.

Eve had to believe he wasn't as pleased with his plans as he wanted her to think. Maybe she wasn't the only one with a crush.

Outside a glimmer of sun broke through the clouds as if proclaiming it a true eureka moment. Even if she was wrong, Eve realized she wasn't ready to give up on Trey. He pulled at her and she wanted to know why.

A professional sounding knock echoed from the front of the house. She imagined the person it belonged to hadn't wanted to sound too timid or overeager. Eve looked at the clock. She gave the kid one mental point for punctuality and grabbed another mug for her guest before going to let him in.

With a handshake and please-come-in combo, Eve led the young man, Thomas, back to the kitchen and tried not to worry over the multiple earrings he sported. "I've got coffee brewing if you'd like or..."

"Coffee, please," he said before she could finish. "I haven't had my second cup yet."

Coffee-lover, too. Eve gave him another check mark on the scoreboard in her head and gave him a more intense once-over. His brown hair was long in front, but neatly trimmed. He had manners, yet didn't appear to be overly nervous. Serious hazel eyes waited for her to throw the ball back to his side of the court.

She set his cup in front of him and gestured to the creamer and sweeteners that sat in the middle of the island then sat on the stool she had strategically positioned opposite his. The kitchen was a good spot for the interview, but she wanted a bit of distance to keep it business-like.

"I understand you have some banquet experience?"

Thomas whipped out a resume from a brown binder and handed it over. "I've worked as a server in both restaurant and banquet settings. I have experience in training, and I also bartend."

"Training?"

He pointed to a bullet on the paper still lying face up between them. "Trainer for new employees at Marco's Italian Cuisine."

Eve was both surprised and impressed as she looked over his resume. He had qualifications in most of the areas she was concerned about. The position might develop into a full-time assistant in the future, depending on his performance and revenue generated in the first few months.

"Do you cook at all?" Eve asked.

He looked pained and shook his head. "And I'd rather not, if that's okay with you."

Point number three. "It's absolutely okay with me." Eve sipped her own coffee and relaxed. "I tend to be a little territorial in the kitchen."

Things went smoothly after that, with a promise from Eve that she would check his references and call him back that afternoon. And assurance from Thomas that the earrings, or piercings as he had clarified, would come out for any job or customer contact.

After he'd left and Eve had fixed herself some lunch of roast beef and cheddar on sourdough, she got back to work and started making those calls. While speaking to the second person she'd needed to phone, she heard a beep in her ear and pulled her cell away to see who was trying to get through. It was Trey.

She couldn't break off to answer but quickly wound up the conversation she was having with a former manager of Thomas's. She needed to take a breath and regroup before talking to Trey anyway.

He'd left the clean dishes on the back porch the day after their disastrous meal, but Eve hadn't seen or spoken to him at all. Tamping down a bubble of excitement, Eve reminded herself they were still in a quasi-business relationship. He was most likely calling about the van.

The phone emitted a little trill in her hand to let her know she had a voice mail.

Sure enough, Trey had left a message and mentioned dropping by to discuss an idea he had about the vehicle. He said he would come by after work and that she should call if that was a bad time for her. Eve looked again at the brushed nickel clock on the wall, a new purchase that went well with her perfect kitchen.

It was still early yet. She had plenty of time to decide how to handle Trey when he showed up.

~~~

Trying desperately to relax, or at least have the appearance of being at ease, Eve flipped the channels on the console television. It was bad enough the screen was so small, compared to modern plasmas, but her grandmother didn't have cable, and Eve hadn't had time to set it up. Number twenty-two on the list of things she'd get to sooner or later.

She settled on a re-run with that crazy redhead who always made her laugh. The expression on the actress's face as she squashed grapes was hysterical, and Eve actually found herself laughing. Before she knew it, Trey was ringing her cell again.

She answered to a brusque, "Hey. I wanted to make sure it was all right before I came over."

"Sure," Eve replied in a tone she felt sounded too chipper. *Easy. Don't want to go too far in the other direction.*

After they hung up, she tried to find the humor in the show again, but was already tensing up. Just two nights ago she'd considered seducing him, and now she was back to square one. Nervous and unsure.

She met him at the door before he could knock and walked back to turn off the T.V. The commercial on now was advertising a local haunted house with all proceeds going to charity, but the sound of ghosts howling and recorded screams were enough to have Eve fumbling with the remote.

A calm hand eased the black controller from her and punched the right button, throwing the room into utter silence. Trey didn't mention Eve's trembling, though he'd obviously noticed, having come to her rescue. He asked instead where he could plug in his laptop.

"If you need the Internet, I'm afraid you're out of luck." She smiled sheepishly. "Nan never saw the attraction."

"Just a power outlet."

"Why don't we go to the sunroom? I could use some light." A second thought occurred to her. "Unless that will make it too difficult to see the screen?"

"No, it should be fine." Trey held out an arm. "Lead the way."

They settled themselves into wicker chairs of golden wood covered with brick red cushions, and Trey opened the computer on the glass table between them. This was one room Eve wouldn't touch. Rarely did her style line up with Nan's, but the Bombay themed sunroom with its looming tropical plants was the exception. It was a place to escape, Nan had explained, and

Eve felt the same way.

"I thought you might want a logo and the name of your business on the side of the van," Trey told her as a blank screen popped up.

Eve considered the idea. "I've got the name, but haven't nailed down a logo. The name will be Classic Catering, nothing too cutesy or long, just direct. What do you think?" It struck her again that she valued his opinion.

"It's fine. I think direct is best."

His tone resonated with double meaning, but Eve was sure it was her imagination.

Clearing her throat, she asked, "So what are you showing me?"

"I'm not showing." He turned the monitor to face her as well as himself. "We are making."

"I don't know how to do any of this." Eve held her hands up in a halting motion.

"We're only brainstorming, and I know you can do that." He flashed her his smile that dared her to back down.

Damn him and those chocolate eyes. "Fine, but don't expect much. I got as far as two Cs linked together."

"Okay. That's a start." His hands typed two Cs in then moved the cursor over a bunch of symbols that meant nothing to Eve until she saw the shape and contour of the letters change with each choice.

"And we can turn the digital image into whatever is needed for the van?" she asked, moving closer.

"I can save it to an SD card and take it to the right guy." He clicked another button and started testing out different colors.

Eve leaned forward to stop his hand when she saw a combination she liked and felt her breast brush against his arm. It burned in a good way, a very good way, and the rest of her responded. "Computers and cars," she said because she could think of nothing coherent and pulled back.

He had stilled when they touched. His eyes burned as he

turned toward her in a controlled movement. "I'm good with things that are low maintenance. I know what to expect and what's expected of me."

It was a warning as much as an invitation. He was willing to go back to where they'd found themselves two nights ago and jump off the ledge into what they both knew would be pure ecstasy. He was ready to take her upstairs and share that with her, but only if she were willing to accept the limitations.

"You can't control everything. Sometimes life gets away from you." Eve could feel the electricity between them. It seemed as frustrated as she was, with nowhere to burn itself out. Oh, how she wanted to ground herself by molding her body to Trey's. To feel the hiss and spit of the energy they would create.

But he'd dug his heels in and was trying to make the rules. Eve wanted more than his strict guidelines, and was sure that part of him did too. He just didn't know it yet.

"I'd like to take some time and think this over." She was referring to more than the logo design and knew he understood.

"Good idea. I know you don't want to commit to anything before you're sure." His eyes raked over her with longing and a patience that was wavering from the fight. "I'll see myself out." He closed up the laptop and left with no further discussion, but gave Eve a nice view of long, muscular thighs walking away. She noticed other attributes that had her cursing her own fortitude.

She wanted to call him back, but with the state they were both in, good sense and wise decisions would be tossed aside. She wouldn't be able to stop herself from agreeing to anything he asked, so she forced herself to breathe and focus on the goal. She knew what she had to do.

A sweetly terrible idea had taken root, and though it might backfire, she felt better risking a little instead of too much or nothing at all.

Eve trailed her hands down her arms to chase away the last of the chills and determined her course of action. She would add one more stop to the next day's to-do list. There was a little something she needed to pick up.

Then she would see just what Trey Rainwater was made of.

TEN

The overhead lighting of the supply store was blinding and cast a sickly pallor over all the items. The place wasn't as nicely set up as the store she and Gabrielle had visited and had few displays, but it made up for that with lower prices and rare goods.

They still managed to decorate for Halloween, though, and Eve felt like the whole world was trying to cram it down her throat. It was October fifteenth. Practically halfway there. She reasoned if she'd already made it through the last eleven days, she could withstand two more weeks.

Being forced to come back to Pine Creek to live was hard. Being thrown into that particular fire during her least favorite month of the year was trial by torture. The stress of starting her own business was actually a blessing and served as a distraction.

Other than the horrible episode she'd had after hearing about the poor college student being murdered, the strange poems, and a gorgeous man that was driving her emotions as wild as he was her hormones...gosh, things were just rosy.

Eve pushed all of that down into her mental lock box and hurried past the red-eyed skulls that mocked her fear and grabbed a bag of strawberry licorice sticks just for spite.

She needed a few more things and would then be on her way to the next and last errand for the day. Unbelievably, she was more excited about the upcoming purchase than any of the platters she'd picked out. And that said a mouthful.

Since she lived to cook, the shift in her priorities meant she had deeper feelings for Trey than she first realized. Or wanted.

As she turned a corner onto aisle number seven, a large brawny man spun at the sound of her footsteps. She wished she had time to retreat, but he had already seen her.

"Now you gotta' go to the same stores as me? You really are a snake."

Fighting the urge to roll her eyes heavenward, Eve grinned tightly. "Sturg. There are only so many specialty stores around here. We're bound to run into each other now and then." Enough was enough with this guy. Could he really be that paranoid? She held up a hand to shield her face. "I promise not to look at what you're buying."

Eyes that were already small enough to disappear into their sockets squinted even harder. "You makin' fun of me?"

Honestly, how could this guy turn out the food he did, which Eve had to admit was pretty good. Maybe that was the tack to take with him. "Yes, I am." She sputtered on before he could work up more mad. "Look, I don't want to interfere with your business, Sturg. In fact, I wanted to tell you how wonderful our lunch was the other day."

He kept silent and Eve could tell he was trying to decide if she was lying.

She glanced down at the cutlery he had been browsing and tapped one of the boxes. "We used these once at the restaurant I used to work for. They didn't hold up well in the washer." She smiled for extra sincerity.

Sturg looked back down at the hardware and grunted. Eve thought this was the best she'd be getting from him today. "Well, nice to see you. Gotta' run." She marched away, determined to put distance between herself and the strange man. Did he treat everyone so badly, or did he save it all for her? It sure felt like he did.

Eve checked out at the register, throwing an occasional glance back for the deli-owning bull, but managed to escape without further harassment. The sun was bright today but was losing its valiant battle against the cold.

She tossed her purchases into the back of her small silver SUV and slipped into the driver's seat, thankful to be out of the bracing wind. A muffled ringtone sang out from the depths of her purse. After locating it, she read the screen, but all it could tell her was that a private number was calling. She answered anyway.

"Eve, it's Kurt Dennis. I wanted to make sure you were settling in and make sure you didn't have any unanswered questions or concerns."

"I'm doing okay, but I appreciate the follow-up," Eve said, switching the phone from her right hand to her left in order to start the ignition and get some heat flowing.

"Good to hear. If you need anything, don't hesitate."

She thought it very out of character for a lawyer to make this kind of call personally, especially since he had already been paid, but Eve took advantage of the moment. "I do have one question. How well do you know Trey Rainwater?"

A pause met her inquiry before Kurt cleared his throat and said, "I don't know him that well, but I understand he spends a good deal of time working. He hasn't been much of a socializer, but is friendly enough. You're not having any problems with him, are you?"

"No, no," she reassured him. "He knew my grandmother, and like you said, he's not all that social. I was just curious about your overall impression."

"That's easy. He's a loner and a hard worker. That's the only impression I could form of him, since it's all I've seen. He's an ex-military man of some sort, I don't know what exactly, but your grandmother did seem to think highly of him, despite his remote attitude."

"My grandmother mentioned him to you?" Eve asked.

"She may have. In passing." He clipped off his words.

Eve definitely sensed hesitancy, but assumed Kurt was busy

and distracted by a more important matter. "Well, thanks again for checking up on me. Everything's going well. Better than I would have imagined, actually."

"I'm glad to hear it." And he sounded like he was. "Again, anytime, just call."

"Thanks." She hung up the phone with a tiny demon on her shoulder telling her something was off. Why would he call and offer to answer any questions she had then turn guarded and evasive? Maybe he didn't feel comfortable discussing other people, a practice he had to adopt for the sake of confidentiality.

That made sense. He was an attorney.

Feeling better, Eve spotted a fast food restaurant that made her favorite sundae and decided to fuel herself up and then her car. With the heater blasting and sunshine beaming down, her spirits were soaring.

She just hoped she was about to make the right choice.

~~~

Lasagna was cooking and its rich aroma filled the air with a promise to satisfy, but Trey doubted the microwavable meal would come close to the real thing. When the wondrous tool of radiation beeped three times, he was still imagining an alternative.

Eve could probably whip up a killer Italian meal with real cheeses and sausage. And look incredibly sexy while doing it. The thought made his mouth water in more ways than one.

He jerked the door open and burned his hand in his haste to remove the little plastic tray, the jolt of pain only adding to his foul mood. He had to stop thinking of Eve or he'd go crazy. He craved the taste of her lips now that he knew they were as soft as they looked. *Never sample the wine when you know you can't afford the bottle.*

He had been off his game since their dinner and didn't know how to repair the damage he'd done or even if he should. One night he decided he was better off leaving her alone, the next thing he knows, he's throwing ultimatums at her feet and praying she chooses the one he wants. To give him everything with no expectations or regrets.

And when did I start giving a damn about not having any particular woman? If the person he was involved with didn't like the scenario he offered, then there was always another who would. He'd never gotten stuck on the idea of pursuing a female unless she was on the same page. Eve Taylor was not only a different book but in an entirely different genre.

It would be easier if he didn't have to see her every day. Watch the light come on in her bedroom at night and wonder what she slept in. If she would spread out on the far side from him or keep one of those gorgeous legs hooked through his.

She's not the only woman in the world with long legs. Move on already.

Braving the vicious little container again, he pulled back the thin cover, careful to avoid escaping steam. He'd been burned one time too many this week.

Two bites and his prediction had come true. It wasn't as good as the real thing but would serve as sustenance so he could get back to work. A hotel in the Swiss Alpine themed town of Helen had contracted with Rainwater Site Design, and there were plenty of other establishments crammed into the hills and valleys of that tourist destination. They might need a website or possibly some improvements to one they already had, so he was doing his best work on this project, all the flash and whistles. A good customer reference was the cornerstone of success.

He was scraping the last bit of sauce out when he heard a knock on the door. He wasn't expecting anyone.

He opened the door to find Eve, holding a large cardboard box with a blue bow and wearing an even bigger smile. She was being no help at all. How was he supposed to get her out of his head when the scent of gardenias was pummeling his inner male into overdrive? He wanted to kiss her.

Hell, he just wanted her.

Sky blue eyes danced with mischief above cheeks pinked by the brisk night air. "I brought you a present." She didn't wait to be invited but moved into the open space between the kitchen and breakfast room where she put the box down.

"Eve. You didn't need to…"

"Oh, I did. I needed to. And you needed me to." She stood there oozing self-satisfaction that put his antennae on alert.

"Hurry and open it," she said.

Baffled and strangely apprehensive, Trey moved toward the box but stopped dead in his tracks when it shook and emitted scratching noises. As a man who prided himself on rarely being caught unaware, he had no clue what to say. Instead, he glowered at the woman before him who could barely contain her excitement and was even now untying the box. She scooped out exactly what Trey had feared was in there.

"It's a puppy," she announced.

He still didn't move. "I see that."

She held the wriggling yellow bundle at arms length and tried to give it to Trey but only succeeded in making him take two steps back for every one she took forward.

"You don't actually think you're going to give me an animal."

She cuddled the dog to her and changed her voice from that of an excited schoolgirl to a teacher explaining something to a willful child. "I know this is an unconventional gift, but I'm doing you a favor."

"I don't want a pet."

"You need a pet. I considered a cat, but that wouldn't suit the purpose. Cats are too low maintenance," she said, throwing his words back at him. Putting the dog down, Eve watched it run, rather unsuccessfully, down the hallway where it tried to make a sharp turn into one of the rooms. Unable to stop its puppy momentum, it *thunked* into the wall instead. Unfazed, the dog righted itself and loped through the first open door it saw.

Eve laughed and turned back to Trey. "Isn't he adorable? I picked a boy. Something told me you would bond more quickly with one of your own."

He ran an aggravated hand through his hair. The woman had lost her mind. "I'm not bonding with anything. Take it back."

"Now see, there's your problem. You said it yourself. You're not bonding with anything, and that obviously includes people, too."

"I'm too busy. I've got a company to run. I don't have time for entanglements, for staying up all night to whining, or running home to take something outside to pee. If it's not housebroken, I don't want it." He strode down the hall after the pup then turned to stalk back to Eve instead. His mind was a riot of turmoil. His life used to be simple. In control and simple.

"I'm housebroken," she said. "And you still don't want me."

"You know I want you." To prove his point and release some of his frustration at the same time, Trey let his anger goad him into grabbing Eve by the arms and pulling her against him. His mouth took hers roughly, invading the softness there with no hint of the gentle kiss they'd shared the last time.

Instead of pushing him away, her arms snaked up to clasp his back. In an instant his plan turned against him, and all he could think of was feeling more of her. He loosened his grip on her arms, letting one hand fall to her hip before it slid around the curve of her backside.

Eve still voiced no objection but moaned sweetly, a sound that drove him wild and had him positioning his thigh between hers. With one swift motion, he pressed himself against the heat of her womanhood and pulled her against him, melding them until he couldn't tell if it was his own throbbing desire he felt or hers.

Eve finally let her head fall forward to bury it in his neck but didn't let go. "Oh, Trey." She breathed against him and placed one wet kiss on his skin before dragging herself out of his arms. "What do you do to me?"

Nothing scripted for an adult film could have turned him on more than those words. Knowing he affected her the same way she did him was more potent than the most lethal of drugs.

"Why won't you let this happen?" he asked.

Eve raised a shoulder. "I can't explain it. I was wary of you from the first time you sneaked up on me in the yard. Now that we know each other better, I can't help feeling there's something between us. It's different, and please don't underestimate how hard it is for me to tell you this, but I can't go any further without you."

"I'm here with you now."

"I don't mean physically. You hold a piece of yourself back, away from the rest of the world, and I...I just feel like you should let it go. One time. With me."

Trey knew he should tell her something reassuring. She was right. Part of him wanted to let go, but the stronger portion of him knew he had to go it alone. He'd battled through jungles to find what others couldn't, and had always done so by himself. He worked best that way. Involving others only meant potential mistakes he would either have to clean up or leave behind.

He stared hard at Eve, knowing there was no way he could explain it to her.

She gave him a reprieve. "Don't say anything. I can see that stubbornness taking over. Just meet me halfway."

Trey sighed, relieved she wasn't going to push him. They kept coming to a stalemate regarding their personal situation, so he was eager to get back to puppy politics and hear what she proposed. "How am I going to do that?"

A scramble of claws fighting for purchase on his hardwood floors drew both of their attention to the blur of golden fuzz racing toward them. The puppy skidded into Trey's boot and seemed content to stay there and gather its wits.

Trey stared down at what appeared to be a golden retriever,

or pretty close to full-blooded. Something about the length of its nose said mutt, and Trey found that he approved. The puppy was all ears, feet, and big brown eyes. Then he yawned and was all mouth.

Trey raised doubtful eyes to Eve. "This is meeting you halfway, right?"

She nodded.

"I know exactly where you're going with this," he warned.

"Then you shouldn't have any trouble avoiding my carefully devised trap." Eve came to him and kissed his cheek before bending to pick up the puppy. It was fighting to stay awake and had worn itself out investigating the premises. She held it out to Trey again.

With a sigh that shook the rafters, he took the dog and held it in the crook of one arm. Its head lolled back onto his shoulder. "So what's the deal? How long do I have to keep it, and when I give it back, where's it going?"

"You keep it until you don't want to anymore." She held up a finger when he opened his mouth to respond. "Nope. As long as it's after this weekend. I've got too much going on right now."

Trey gave what he hoped was a smartass grin. "In that case, I'll be happy to babysit *your* puppy until Monday."

"I'll get its food and bed from my car. Don't go anywhere."

Eve dodged back out into the night, leaving Trey scowling and holding his new roommate. A sound like that of a wheeze mixed with a snort was coming from the dog, and he was already making plans to put the puppy's bed in his garage.

He might not be sleeping with Eve, but he wasn't going to be content with a puppy by his side. Especially one that snored.

Eleven

So far so good, Eve told herself as she checked the layout in the reception room one last time. The bride and her mother had compromised, given the minuscule amount of time they had left Eve to prepare, and agreed on a buffet spread of entrees. Guests would serve themselves from the shiny chafer pans while servers, Joni and Thomas, would circulate with appetizers and champagne.

In addition to having her wedding cakes baked by a specialty bakery, the client had also hired a bartender separately, leaving one less thing for Eve to deal with. She would be busy making sure everything remained adequately filled and performing as troubleshooter extraordinaire.

With the bride and groom closing in on the "I do" portion of the ceremony, Eve smoothed her hands over the pale blue business suit she'd chosen. Along with pearl earrings and hair in an elegant twist, she felt the look was both stylish and professional. Her left lapel sported a silver plate with her name over the words Classic Catering, a little gift she'd given herself at the last minute.

Each table was covered with a white table cloth, and three yellow candles of varying height cast their amber glow from silver plates. A circle of petals, fuchsia and yellow, completed the centerpieces and were lovely in their simplicity.

Weddings always reminded her of hope and fairy tales fulfilled. The little girl in her thrilled at the idea of flouncy white dresses and Prince Charmings come to life. She truly wished every happiness for the young couple and could admit to the mildest of envy whenever the girl spoke of her soon-to-be husband. She seemed to light the world with her happiness.

"Everything's set," Thomas said at her left elbow. "If we run out of champagne, we can direct them to the bar."

Joni joined them. Her two new employees were decked out in black pants and vests with white button downs. They had both argued for full black, but Eve cast the only vote that mattered. That of the boss.

She had also canned Thomas's multiple piercings and the goth make-up Joni was so fond of. With her brown hair pulled back in a ponytail, the girl actually looked her twenty-two years instead of thirty. "If they manage to drink all that champagne, we'll have a drunken mob on our hands," Joni stated. "We're set for an army of party-crashers."

"Then it's as it should be," Eve said with a confident smile. The last two days had been harrowing, and she'd feared something would be left undone. But taking in the glory of accomplishment that surrounded her now, she felt ready for anything.

"Hey, did you hear they found that guy's body?" Joni asked Thomas.

Anything but that.

"No kidding. Where?" Thomas returned, his hazel eyes widening in shock. "My brother knew him. They graduated together."

"What are you talking about?" Eve finally asked, though she had a curl of dread forming in her chest. Today was a day of new beginnings, and she hated to have the joy of the occasion dampened by anything sinister.

"A man disappeared earlier this week. He was at some bar in another town close to here and that was the last anyone saw of him." Joni pushed square-framed glasses more firmly onto her nose. "His girlfriend reported him missing."

"But that was just last night, my brother told me. And now

they've already found him?" Thomas said with disbelief, and Eve wondered how good a friend the dead man had been to his brother.

"Was he in an accident?" Eve hoped it was so, though it made her feel guilty to be thinking selfish thoughts about a person's untimely death.

"Doubt it. Considering he was found out in the woods." Joni jerked a thumb over her shoulder in the direction of the tiny room where their personal things were stored. "I've still got the paper if you want to read it."

Mandy's crooked version of the story, no doubt. "Not now." Eve tried for a diversion. "Let's do one more list check. The ceremony will be over soon, and it's easy to feel prepared when there aren't a hundred people swarming to fill their stomachs."

"Aye-aye, cap'n." Joni gave a limp salute and started her rounds while a quiet Thomas headed to the kitchen. Eve could see why the girl got along so well with Gabrielle. They were two quirky peas in a pod.

Trying to dismiss the flicker of worry in the back of her mind, Eve walked to the large wooden doors painted purity white that led from the church hallway and into the banquet room. She opened them for a more welcoming feel, since guests would soon start to trickle in.

With little to do but wait, she again felt a stab of apprehension. Two people had been found murdered. She had received two strange poems. There was no obvious connection, but something was dancing in the depths of her memory. She struggled to think of what was bothering her when she looked up to see Joni and Thomas lingering in the kitchen doorway, ready for action.

That was it. The first poem had definitely been addressed to a female, and Eve now had to believe it was her. The second poem had her name on the outside of the envelope, but her brief perusal of the script gave her a different impression than the first. She had only read it once. It had made little sense, so she'd quickly banished it to a drawer in her grandmother's old roll top desk.

Now she distinctly remembered it used the word "he." The masculine reference is what made her bridge her poems to the murders. First a woman then a man. *Ridiculous. Sheer coincidence. Do not let your freak-filled imagination ruin this.*

Bursts of laughter and boisterous conversation were welcome sounds as they drew closer. It seemed her client was now a married woman, and here came Eve's first real job as a caterer. She was determined the reception be nothing short of exemplary.

With a deep breath and clasped hands, she rounded to face Joni and Thomas. "Okay. Here we go."

~~~

The last of the heavy items had been moved inside to the pantry, which Eve had re-shelved during the renovations to make better use of the large space. Thomas had volunteered to follow her home and help unload, so she'd added a little more to his payment.

The wedding had gone well, other than an unexpected run on some of the hors d'oeuvres. The fee paid to Classic Catering wouldn't quite cover the cost of ingredients, supplies, and what she'd paid Joni and Thomas, but the chafer dishes and other purchases would be used again and again.

A lone bird had been serenading Eve as she unloaded and gave one last cry before bursting from its hiding place among the branches of a large pin oak. She watched it soar to a phone pole across the street and resettle. It was a large black bird, possibly a crow. She recalled a report from school on the symbolism of birds in literature, certain the cawing observer would have been used to represent a bad omen.

Its dark silhouette against a sky of indigo and racing silver clouds made Eve shiver. Even more ominous was the bird's sudden silence. She would swear something or someone was out there in the night. Watching her.

The rush of a car passing by startled her back into action. She'd spooked herself and wanted nothing more than to tuck away safely inside and end the busy day with a hot bubble bath and glass of chardonnay. Her muscles needed the soak and her mind needed the calm.

After locking herself in and setting the last two bags on the floor, where she would leave them until the morning, Eve was struck by the notion that she truly felt like she was coming home. She didn't miss her little apartment, the restaurant she'd managed, or the neighbors she'd never really gotten to know very well.

Here she was known, for the good as well as the bad. Her family had deep roots in this red earth. She'd branched out and seen some of the world for herself but had ended up back in the hills and valleys of Georgia. Against her will.

For the first time, Eve felt an inkling of gratitude for her grandmother's crafty maneuver. Maybe Nan really had known best.

Dropping her purse on the bottom step and coat over the banister, Eve climbed the stairs with the easy movements of a woman overrun by exhaustion but sustained by contentment. She was thinking lavender for the bath, and candles. Nice and soothing.

Remembering the wine, she stopped and grudgingly turned to head back down when a clunk from below brought her up short. She stayed where she was, frozen but listening for any telltale sound. Her mind raced furiously, trying to identify anything in the house that could account for what she'd heard.

The bags, she thought and managed to breathe in and relax, the aftershocks of fear running through her veins until her heart released and began to slow. There were unused sternos in the bags, and one of the little fuel canisters probably tumbled around and hit the floor. The more she thought about it, the more sure she became.

Chiding herself for being so jumpy, Eve traversed the few steps to the bottom where she kicked off her heels, adding to the items accumulating there. In the morning. She'd take care of everything in the morning.

Her bare feet padded across chilly wood floors making her stop to raise the temperature on the thermostat. She would have frozen once she'd undressed and imagined herself making a naked dash through the house to turn up the heat.

The bottle of wine was where she'd left it, and she took great pleasure in retrieving one of her glasses with the colorful spiral stems. They were different, fun and female, and exactly what she was in the mood for. Taking a long drink she emptied the glass halfway, then refilled for her leisurely soak in the tub.

Another noise drew her eyes toward the front of the house. It had been low, a scrape and squeak of someone trying to move silently. Someone unaware of the loose board near the porch steps. She lowered the glass, but her stare was riveted on the foyer.

A shaft of yellow fell from the hallway light and partially covered the area. It was difficult to see through the stained glass, but in one painful space of her heartbeat, Eve saw a shift of movement behind it.

Someone was standing on the other side of her front door.

She glanced at the phone on the wall, considering a call to nine-one-one, but was overcome by an instinct to run. To get away. She could make it out the back and into the yard, but if he heard her, there was still the chance of being chased down and caught.

Trey. He had to be home. If the stranger on her doorstep gave chase, she would scream. And Trey would hear.

Afraid to lose any more time and give the man a chance to change his location, Eve threw open the bolt on the back door and slid out, not bothering to close it behind her. She crept across the back porch and took the steps on her tiptoes, careful not to make a sound.

There were no lights on at Trey's. Maybe he was in bed or on the other side of the house. *Please be there.*

Panic was swelling in her throat, and the rush of her own blood filled her ears with a roar. Or maybe it was the rising wind that tossed leaves in a swirl behind her. Terror would not be held at bay and began pushing through to suffocate her, like a clawed hand squeezing the breath from her lungs.

The crow from earlier let out a loud caw, and Eve swore he was warning her to run. Warning her the beast was on her trail.

She lurched into movement, racing over fallen branches and acorns that cut her feet. Her voice wouldn't work at first, only a rasp and moving lips, then she found the strength to scream Trey's name once, and again with more desperation.

She tried to focus on his house, but the edges of the world were growing bleary. Distance was no longer measurable. The bird, the trees, the horrible yellow moon were all there. Clearly there. But they began to fade, and the shape of another place, another time, started to appear.

No, please. Not now.

Images of the past and present began to blur and spin, driving her to her knees and onto the cold, dew-covered carpet of leaves. She couldn't get up again with the dizziness swamping her. She could only throw one last pleading look toward the towering white house next door.

A light was on. Had it been there before? Gasping in a breath for one last call for help, Eve prayed she would be heard in time.

The cry never passed her lips. Large hands came from behind, followed by arms that tightened and encircled her with a strength she couldn't fight or break free of.

That she couldn't escape.

Twelve

She was so pale, lying there on the couch. Pale as death, or something very close to it, with a blue and white wedding-ring quilt thrown over her for warmth.

Trey worried he should be calling someone, her brother or Gabrielle, someone used to dealing with this. He delayed the phone calls, because he was also sure Eve would want him to keep what happened as quiet as possible.

What did happen? What were you running from, Eve?

Falling back on one of his mother's comfort measures, he went to the kitchen, intent on making some hot tea for when Eve awoke. Somehow coffee didn't seem right.

He took a moment to appreciate her new work space with its rich brown counters and ivory cabinetry. It suited her, he thought, stylish and sophisticated with a welcoming vibe that made him feel at home. It was a place to sit and chat about things both important and trivial, and Trey could easily picture himself here with Eve, sharing a light dinner after work or making waffles on a Sunday morning.

And it was enough to shake him to the tips of the hiking boots he'd shoved on when he'd heard her scream. He'd been nodding off on his own couch, watching a movie where most everything was being blown up, when the sound of his name pierced through the night, even past the commotion pounding from his surround sound.

His heart had crowded into his throat, and he still felt as hollowed out as she looked. He'd killed men before, because it had been his life or theirs. Over time, he'd hardened and chosen to keep a measure of distance between himself and the things of this world that were unreliable, that might bring danger or pain. He was still surviving, even in the civilian world, and human relationships were nothing if not unreliable.

Yet seeing Eve crumpled to the ground, mumbling incoherently, had pierced him with the coldest of blades. At that moment, saving her was all that mattered.

The shiny red kettle whistled from the stove. Trey removed it from the burner and turned off the gas flames before pouring the scalding water over two tea bags in identical white mugs. There was surely some contraption in here that would have done the job more quickly, but he needed the ritual as well as the warmth.

He felt slightly emasculated but fixed a serving tray with cream and sweeteners, so Eve wouldn't have to get off the couch. Butlering wasn't in his normal repertoire, but the need to bring solace to the woman in the other room overrode male pride. It looked like the chef had been too busy to cook for herself the last few days, if the bakery box in the corner was any indication. Lifting the lid, he picked a couple of blueberry scones to add to his presentation. His ego could stand it.

Carrying it all into the living room, he noticed Eve's lids at mid-mast before they flicked open with a jolt. She was awake, and myriad emotions boiled beneath her outer calm. She studied him for a moment as if unsure who he was, then heaved a great sigh. "Trey. You came." Her hands rubbed over the quilt then squeezed. "I'm home."

Trey wondered if it was a statement or clarification. He set the tray on the coffee table. There would be plenty of time for questions. "What do you want in your tea?"

Eve pushed herself up to a sitting position and studied the display. "You made tea?" Putting a hand to her mouth, she furrowed her brow before asking, "How long was I out?"

"About twenty minutes. I found you in the yard and carried

you in."

"Yes, that part I remember. I was running to you..." Alarm raced across her features as she swiveled her head to check the room. "Is he gone? Did you see him?"

A new level of concern shrouded the night, and the man who had just served tea and scones was replaced by someone entirely different. If people held any semblance of primal reactions in their DNA, then Trey was experiencing what a wolf might in the instant his mate was threatened. He could practically feel hairs standing at alert and teeth baring themselves with the thirst for flesh.

"Who, Eve? Was someone here?"

He knew she saw the transformation when she placed a hand on his arm, comfort meant for him or herself. "There was someone on the porch. I was in the kitchen, and there was a noise before."

"It's okay. Whoever it was is gone now, and you're safe." Trey could see the panic flaring to life again, and he needed her to stay calm. He needed to know everything.

Everything.

"We should call the police," he said, starting to rise.

"No. Wait." She licked her lips and grabbed him with both hands now. "Please. We can do that in the morning. We can leave things the way they are and let them look around in the daylight. I just can't do it now. I can't answer questions."

He sat down again and handed her the tea she still hadn't picked up, curling her hands around the glass to warm her fingers. His hands stayed over hers for a moment. "Okay. We'll wait until morning. But for now, what do you want in your tea?"

She half sobbed, half-smiled. "I'll do it." She reached for a spoon and a little blue packet. "Would you check to make sure the doors are locked?"

Trey made his rounds, double checking locks and pulling curtains to block out any prying eyes. He wasn't sure what was happening here but wasn't foolish enough to risk Eve or her state of mind. She needed to feel safe.

Eve was making a second cup of tea when he returned and set some kindling and logs in the fireplace. They weren't going anywhere for a while, and he wanted to make sure she relaxed.

Once the crackle and roar of the fire permeated the room with its warmth and hypnotic flickering, Trey sat on the opposite end of the couch from Eve. He wanted to give her space but stay close enough for contact.

He watched her as she stared into the cup like a mystic looking for the future. "Eve." Her gaze rose slowly to him. "When I found you out there, you were more than scared and passed out as soon as you were in my arms. Based on what I've seen and what I know, I think there's more to it than fear of an intruder."

She visibly tightened, fingers turning white with their grip on the cup. "You don't believe me?"

"I believe you," Trey said calmly, "but I know that's not all there is to it. The state you were in out there was like what happened to you the other day. You came to me when you were in trouble, now you're blocking me out again. Why can't you trust me?"

She set the tea aside and clasped her hands, head lowered. Here was a woman full of doubt, and if he didn't know any better, full of shame. "You read the article, so you know what happened," she whispered.

"Sketchy details, but you don't have to talk about that. I'm more concerned with the shaking, terrified woman I saw on the cold, hard ground because she didn't know where she was."

"You're right. I got lost, and it happens sometimes. It's because of what happened that Halloween. I won't go into all the details, but for you to understand the episodes, I have to explain." Eve bent her knees and tucked her feet under herself, a self-protective motion. She was shoring up, and Trey appreciated how hard this must be for her. "You know I was taken by a man, a monster, and held captive for days."

He nodded.

"What the article didn't say, what no one can really comprehend, was the impact those days had on an eight-year-old girl's mind. Not that I'm not grateful. Others weren't as lucky as me." She reached a shaky hand out for her cup and drank deeply before continuing. "Since the day I was rescued, I've had trouble forgetting. At first it was nightmares and memories too fresh to be forgotten. I carried the darkness around with me in the broad daylight for weeks. My parents got me a therapist, and over time, I learned how to lock it away and forget."

"You had to learn to live again, go on with your life, but some things stay with you." Trey understood recovering from tragedy, the evil and violence people were capable of, but a child's world would be destroyed, discolored forever by a sickening fog of anxiety. Constant fear must have been her shadow. Where was the next bad man? Would she be safe in her own bedroom? Would her family die like the others she'd seen?

"I had support. My parents, Nan. Even Lance and Gabrielle, children themselves, somehow knew I needed them. I was too afraid to leave the house and couldn't go near the school. That's where he found us."

She lifted her head once and gave a slow blink to acknowledge his surprise. "Yeah, you'd think it would be safe there, most people did, and that's why they weren't watching closely enough. There was an old armory across the street, where the Halloween carnival was set up every year. The huge stone building made a great haunted house, and the grounds outside held a maze of cardboard covered in black plastic. There were games, bobbing for apples, the whole works."

The memory of it was evidently too much as Eve stilled and suddenly looked ill.

Trey moved closer and rested a hand on her shoulder, kneading the tension there. "You should stop. We can talk more after you eat."

"I can't think about that place. I never can, but I want to tell you more." She lifted a shoulder and eased her cheek down, squeezing his hand against her face before lowering it and holding it between hers. "I left Pine Creek as soon as I was done with my home-schooling. The attacks were controlled, but I needed to get away. I needed to be somewhere new. Somewhere clean. I hardly ever have them anymore, as long as I stay away from anything or anyplace that might trigger a memory. When that happens, it's like I'm there again, with the man and the other children."

"But you've had two since I've known you," Trey said.

"Three since I came back to Pine Creek to stay."

Damn them all and damn me, too for making her come back to this hell. The truth about Trey's role in her situation almost came roaring off his tongue until Eve spoke.

"That's not the only reason I'm so on edge. I'd say I'm doing pretty well, all things considered."

"The murder." Trey remembered how Gabrielle and Lance had told her of the college student's death right before Eve had one of her episodes. Something she hadn't wanted him to see.

A wry smile touched her lips then vanished. "Two murders now, and I've also been getting some strange notes. Poems. I think they might be connected to the deaths, but I'm not sure. I received the first one just before the girl was kidnapped, but I didn't think anything of it until today."

Trey's hackles rose again with a fury. "Why?"

"I found out there was a man who disappeared nearby and was found dead. The second note referenced a male." She shrugged. "It just seemed to click."

"I need to see them." Trey took Eve's face in his hands. "But first, I'm going to go lock up my house. Will you be all right for a few minutes?"

"Yes." She looked confused.

He left and got her purse from the steps where he'd noticed

it sitting before. "Your phone in here?" At her answering nod, he dropped it beside her on the quilt. Call me if anything seems out of the ordinary. But I should only be a few minutes."

"What are you going to do?"

Trey gave Eve his best don't-even-think-of-arguing stare. "I'm going to grab a few things and be right back. You're not staying here alone."

Thirteen

They hadn't talked about the poems or anything else the night before, because Eve had fallen asleep. Sitting up and rubbing her face, she realized it was morning, she was in her own bed, and the house smelled of sizzling bacon mixed with something sweeter.

She changed to a pair of her pajamas, as she was still dressed in her suit, and pulled on her favorite fuzzy socks, explosion pink, before meandering downstairs to see who was about.

Trey was standing at the stove, looking a bit panicked, and checking the sides of her waffle-maker. "No steam," he said, still unaware of her presence. "Not done yet." He went back to the bacon and flipped it.

Eve marveled at how he was taking everything in stride after she'd bared her soul and most closely guarded secret. He didn't think she was crazy, and he hadn't run away. In fact, he'd insisted on coming back to be with her. Evidently to cook waffles.

And he'd brought the puppy.

The yip and scramble of claws finally drew Trey's attention to Eve as the puppy danced around her feet sniffing with delight. "I wouldn't get him too excited if I were you," he warned. "Still has some trouble controlling the pipes."

"What? Oh," Eve said, after spotting the yellow drops. "Yuck."

Trey tossed her a bunch of paper towels. "Here you go. You get used to it." Then to the dog. "Don't you, Max?"

"Max?"

Trey wrinkled his brow. "I couldn't keep calling him, 'Hey-Stop-That.'"

"Sure," Eve replied with a grin, but too low for him to hear. She didn't want to rock a boat when it was floating just fine.

"I couldn't leave him at my place. He doesn't like to be alone." He gave her a dirty look. "Something I found out the first night you left him with me."

"Disturbed your sleep, did he? But we probably wouldn't have heard him way over here."

"Well, I didn't want him to tear anything up."

Uh-huh, Eve thought smugly.

Trey focused again on the silver square emitting the glorious smell that just begged for butter and syrup. "Will you check this thing? I'm afraid I'm burning it."

She took a plate then opened the waffle maker. "Looks perfect." She forked the waffle out, wiped down the machine, and re-filled it with batter. "I'll slice some bananas and strawberries, and God bless you," she finished, spying the full pot of coffee.

They worked together in silence then shared their meal and the morning paper Trey had retrieved before she woke. The breakfast nook just to the side of the kitchen was bathed in cool lemon from the distant autumn sun. They sat on the taupe cushions of the corner benches.

There was no pressure to make small talk, and Eve felt completely comfortable, even with her finger-combed hair and PJs. Last night's crisis was all but a distant nightmare, and she wondered how she could feel so rested. So at ease.

Trey gathered their well-used plates and set them in the sink before pouring some more coffee for them both. He sat back down with a look that told her the vacation from reality was over.

"We should call the police, but I'd like to read the letters first."

"Right." Eve ambled into the parlor, her system still waiting on the caffeine-jolt, and removed the notes from the desk. Returning, she let them fall on the table in front of Trey. Touching them was loathsome, because they actually felt dirty.

Eve drank her coffee greedily, hoping the brew might possess power to purge evil. There was a smudge on their perfect morning now, but the issue of the trespasser, probably the unknown author as well, could no longer be brushed aside.

She nabbed a few more slices of berry. No reason it had to be all bad.

"I see what you mean," Trey said, leaning back against the seat but still staring at the orange papers. "The first uses the word fair so often, it has to be about a woman. Plus, it says 'Can compare to you,' as if it literally meant you, Eve."

"After seeing my name on the second envelope, I have to believe that's the case. Guess he was afraid I was dense and missed it the first time."

"You're not dense." Trey slugged some from his own mug. "The second is still vague, and definitely mentions a male, but still seems like the writer was talking to you, telling you something specific."

"But neither of them has anything to do with me."

"No," he agreed. "But don't they remind you of something?"

"Of what exactly?" Eve remembered the words "ebony hair" from the first poem. The reference had triggered something, but it got lost in the back of her mind. That same phrase tickled at her now as if teasing her to recall its meaning.

"Not sure." Trey slid out of the booth to pick up a computer bag in the hallway then set up his laptop between them on the table. "Let's find out."

Eve let him go at it, tapping on the keyboard in search of any clue to the message someone was trying to send her. Who would be interested in a game like this? Who would want to hurt her? And there was no longer any doubt in her mind that whoever was doing this had nothing but cruel intentions.

"Here," Trey said with a slap of one hand on the table. "I knew it was referring to something specific. I remember something about this from college." He swung the computer around so they could both see the screen then handed her the second poem, the one that had been taped to her window. "Read it again."

"I'd rather not," Eve grumbled.

Trey lifted one side of his mouth but touched her hand with a quick brush of encouragement. "Humor me."

She read silently.

> *No Castiaglo is he*
> *I am more him*
> *As you are she*

It still meant nothing to Eve, and she shook her head before tossing the letter back down. "So what is it?"

"I got a hit, and *Castiaglo* is the name of a story about an Egyptian magician."

"Say that three times fast," Eve said, trying to find some humor in the muck.

"Not today, thanks." Trey went on as if she hadn't spoken. "He injected himself with nitrates and became immortal." He stopped and frowned.

"Go ahead. You can't quit now, and I can handle it." Eve hoped she was right, because Trey's face told her he didn't like what he read.

"The magician went around killing women." He looked at Eve. "Women who reminded him of the one who had betrayed him."

Eve sighed. "Then that has nothing to do with me, because I've never betrayed anyone."

Trey looked unconvinced. "Are you sure this might not be an ex-boyfriend or ex-lover? Maybe he's not happy you moved away from him."

"I'm sure."

"Think hard. Anyone you might have turned down or broken away from?"

She left him sitting alone and went to load the dirty dishes into the washer. She needed something to keep her hands busy. "You make it sound like this is somehow my fault." She dropped a plate in with a clang.

"I didn't say that." He looked calm, and Eve wondered what was jousting around inside that too-handsome head of his.

"You didn't say otherwise, either." Maybe the anger was misdirected, but she should be able to say something once and not be told to re-check her facts. "I said I'm sure. I never read Castiaglo, and I don't know what that poem means any more than the first one."

"Okay. We'll move on." He went to work on the computer again but spoke aside to her. "I just need to know what I'm dealing with."

"You mean what I'm dealing with."

At that he stood and strode over to her, facing her down. "I should have said *we*. We are handling this together, right? I came for you last night, and I'm not just going to walk away."

Eve felt a liquid warmth in her eyes and knew she was wavering. Still, she let him gather her against him, felt the stroke of his hand down her back.

Trey whispered against her hair. "I'm not going anywhere yet. Even if you ask me to."

Sniffling and mustering up a smile, Eve pulled back and patted her hair self-consciously. "In other words, I'm stuck with you until you don't want to be stuck anymore? How is it you always manage to lay down the guidelines?"

He looked like he wanted to say something but changed his mind and reverted to safer territory. "We'll figure this out." He chucked her chin. "The first poem is about a fairy tale."

That roused her curiosity. "Which one?"

"Ebony hair. Fair skin." When she continued to stare at him, perplexed, he said, "The fairest of them all."

Eve rolled her eyes and threw her hands up. "Of course. I knew it sounded like I'd heard it before. Snow White." She gave a sharp laugh of relief. At least one riddle was solved.

Then just as quickly, the light slid out of her and was replaced with swirling tendrils of fear. No, it couldn't be that. It was just a coincidence. The poem was nothing more than an allusion to beauty.

Trey steadied her with his strong hands. "Eve, what's wrong? You look like you've seen a ghost."

Unable to speak, she only moved her head in denial. "We have all we're going to get from these letters. Let's bring the cops in."

Eve watched him walk to the wall phone and dial. He was so confident and sure, his body language that of a man who held terror at bay, met danger head on. She was glad he was here, for so many reasons, but still she continued to tremble.

She hadn't seen a ghost, but she'd remembered a monster.

~~~

"You didn't catch a glimpse of his face? Hair color?" The younger of the two detectives in Eve's living room probed her with persistence but managed to sound and look bored. "Anything at all?"

"I told you. I only saw movement. There was a person at my front door, but I couldn't describe him." Eve felt like a child being chastised, though how he managed it without a trace of emotion on his thin face she couldn't tell.

His dark hair was slicked back to reveal a contoured structure any male model would envy. In fact, his manicured hands and sense of style left her to wonder if that hadn't been his previous career. Alan Reston's appearance did not scream "detective."

His partner, on the other hand.

"How do you know it was definitely a male?" the older man asked. Lee Curtis was his name, and though his face was also impassive, his darting eyes took in every detail. They fell on Eve now with hypnotic power as if judging the reliability of his one and only witness.

"I could just tell, by his shape and size."

Detective Curtis moved to stand by the door. "Where did he reach?" He jerked his head toward the stained glass, and Eve saw the sense in his manner of questioning. Indirect, but posed in a way that jarred the previous night back into clarity for her.

"A couple inches over the red panes there." She pointed, remembering all too well the shock of horror when she'd realized someone was there. Waiting or listening. Watching.

Detective Curtis held his hand up to his own black hair, buzzed closely to the scalp and silver at the temples. "Here?"

Eve nodded.

"Then we're looking at about five-eleven or six feet, as I'm just over that." He jotted a note on a small spiral notebook, like they did in the movies.

Eve felt as if her life had become a feature film on how many unbelievable things could go wrong. *Let's wrap it up under two hours folks, and give it a catchy name like, "Home for Hell Month."*

"If your office doesn't believe what's happening to Eve is connected to the murders, why are two detectives here?" Trey finally broke into the conversation, after letting the police have their say and broke Eve out of her bizarre imaginings about weekend specials.

"Because you mentioned the deaths, and we're obliged to follow up on any leads." He held a hand up when Trey crossed his arms in battle stance. "Now, that doesn't mean the department is going to look the other way about Ms. Taylor's trouble. Officers are taking prints and photos as we speak, and we'll have a specialist go over the letters. I'm afraid all we can do at the moment is advise you both to exercise caution and awareness in your daily routines."

"Thank you both for your time," Alan Reston said to Eve and Trey before giving his partner one last bland look before sailing out with the grace of a star on the catwalk.

Eve smirked as she watched him go, but her inner laughter died when she turned to meet kindness in the eyes of Detective Curtis. His face softened. "I remember the night they found you, and I'm sorry you have a stranger invading your life again."

She was stunned by his direct words, yet they were a lifesaver tossed to her in an angry ocean of waves. Here was someone who could understand what she'd seen, because he had, too. Even though it had only been aftermath, the bloody carnage left behind was enough to permanently wound a person's consciousness.

"Looks like you're making a good life for yourself here." He glanced at Trey and back at Eve. "Don't let anyone take it from you." He held up his notebook with a shake as he backed out and through the door into the light. "Let me know if you think of anything else, and I'll make sure it gets to the right people."

The detective pivoted just in time to bump into a frantic Gabrielle as she raced up the porch steps. He excused himself and left.

"Eve. Thank the spirits." Gabrielle rushed to Eve and wrapped her up in a hug. "What is going on? I thought I'd drop in to hear all about the wedding, and I roll up to police cars."

Eve dropped to the floral sofa then thumped it as it squeaked in protest. "I have to replace this thing." She raised an exhausted and pained expression to her friend. "Can I give you the nutshell version?"

"Okay."

"I got another note, and someone was on the porch last night. I freaked out and ran, freaked out some more, then Trey found me and brought me home and spent the night." Eve blew her hair out of her face. "This morning we called the police because we thought the notes, the intruder, and the recent murders were all related, but they aren't."

For the first time Eve could recall, her friend's mouth was open, but the usual rush of witty dialogue was absent.

"Got all that? Good, because I need to eat something." Eve slicked her hands through the flowing gold of her hair then scooped it up into a sort of loose wrap with a band she'd pulled out of her blue-jeaned pocket. "Scratch that. I need to cook something."

Gabrielle shot shrewd eyes to Trey. "Okay, barring all the rest, did she say you spent the night?"

He actually laughed, and the sound was like a back rub to Eve's nervous mood. She rolled her shoulders and chuckled to herself when she heard him say, "Don't go placing any curses on me or anything. I slept on the couch."

"Probably why it's squeaking," Eve interjected. She was in the pantry now, running through ideas of what she was in the mood for. It needed to be something spicy and colorful. She wanted to cook food that all but stood up and told you its name, not only for the eating but for the joy of creating. Fun food.

Chicken fajitas. That was the ticket. And she'd pair it with a Greek salad and crème brulee. She was mixing cultures but didn't care, because the only person she needed to please right now was herself. "You two are staying for lunch," she said with a finger shake that dared them to refuse.

"Great. Fine." Gabrielle tossed her luggage-sized purse into the breakfast nook. "Then you can tell me all about how I'm not supposed to worry about you and stalkers and serial killers. Peachy."

Gabrielle surveyed the kitchen as Trey settled onto a stool. She finally nudged past Eve and grabbed a bag of salt and vinegar chips. "I knew you'd have some of these."

"Hey, not before the feast. I don't want you to get full," Eve protested.

"Puh-lease." Gabrielle tossed the bag to Trey and opened the refrigerator to get out a diet drink. "When she's in this kind of mood," she told him, "you can expect it to be an all-day affair."

Eve noticed the glint in Trey's eye and knew he was enjoying the interruption. She was grateful for the distraction as well and surprised at how excited she was to have Trey and Gabrielle get to know each other. A few quality hours with them, food, and drink would be a balm to her fractured state of mind.

She also liked that Trey wasn't doing his usual escape routine. In fact, he hadn't left her side since the few minutes he'd gone home last night to get his things.

That reminded her of the puppy, and she put a finger to her lips, indicating Gabrielle should be quiet, and motioned for her friend to follow her to the sunroom. She pointed out the fuzzy bundle asleep on its bed and grabbed Gabrielle's hand when her friend moved to pick him up.

"Oh, no," Eve whispered. "With this one, we really do need to let sleeping puppies lie. He'll be plenty affectionate when he wakes up."

When they re-joined Trey in the kitchen, Gabrielle sighed. "I guess the great idea I had is now completely inappropriate. It would have been so much fun, too."

"What was that?" Trey asked, sipping a beer he'd brought from his house, one of the few emergency supplies he'd dragged over along with the dog, a change of clothes, and his toothbrush.

"I just had a brainstorm about how to introduce more people to Eve's culinary talent, but with what's happened, and…"

"Tell me." Eve interrupted her friend's stalling. She was thinking of the detective's parting words, and he was right. She'd had enough of crawling into corners and hiding from the boogeyman.

Then she looked at Trey, the quiet strength in his posture, the fire of defense she'd seen when he'd been there in her darkest, weakest moments. He was something worth fighting for. And so, Eve realized, was she.

She didn't just want to live. She wanted to have a *life*.

"You should maybe throw a party." Gabrielle looked

uncertain, wincing with one side of her face as if expecting an explosion.

"A party." Eve tasted the word like an exotic delicacy of chocolate covered insects she wasn't sure how she felt about yet. Her emotions rolled from excited to cautious and back again. She pursed her lips and narrowed her eyes, deciding to go for the thrill despite any bitterness. "That is exactly right."

Gabrielle widened her brown eyes. "Huh? Don't you want to take some time to think about it?"

"Think about what, Gab? Seriously." Eve was pacing now, every step full of vengeance and hope. "I should waste a few more hours of my life imagining what was done to me? To them? I'm sick of being afraid I might lose it and start seeing things that aren't there. That are in fact long gone. Long dead."

She stopped and slammed a fist onto the island, causing Gabrielle to jump and Trey to grin with a mix of surprise and satisfaction. He looked damn well pleased, and Eve couldn't contain the smile of victory that rose on her own face to meet his.

And she wasn't done yet.

"A Halloween party." She could almost feel her spine strengthening as she stood there. She felt like a newborn superhero.

"Have you lost your mind or are you drunk, because the Eve I know would never carve a pumpkin, much less have a day of the freakin' dead party." Gabrielle's face was growing heated. She was not happy with the turn of events and likely confused.

"If I'm going to exorcise some demons, then I might as well get it done as one big bash. Maybe a stranger stepping his unwanted ass onto my porch, my grandmother's home, was some sort of catalyst. All I know is that I feel the need to beat my chest or sprinkle on the perimeter of my territory. Something like that." She gave a jerk of her head for punctuation. "Hmph."

"Well, give me a heads-up as I'd like to see any of the above," Trey said.

Gabrielle fluttered her hands in the air. "How can you joke? Am I the only one with any sense left? You did say murders, right? *Murders*. That might have something to do with you?"

Because she could see her friend's concern, Eve settled back into gathering utensils and calmed her voice. "I'm not a little girl anymore, and I won't cloister myself away like I did back then."

At the reminder of her friend's broken childhood and days when she couldn't pull Eve out to play, even in the bright, innocent summer sunshine, Gabrielle paused, likely remembering the misery that was now fueling Eve's tirade. "I know. This is just all so sudden." She sighed. "But if your mind's made up, I'll help with whatever you want."

Gabrielle cast a sidelong glance to Trey. "And so will you, since I think you're somehow responsible for this."

He winked at her and lifted his beer before smirking. "Is that a bad thing?"

Eve watched her friend lift a dubious brow before saying with both sugar and arsenic, "I haven't decided yet."

Fourteen

Eve took a big black marker out of its usual drawer and performed her daily ritual by marking through the date. It was October twenty-fourth, and she was almost home free. One more week until Halloween.

And tonight would serve as the final dress rehearsal.

She'd sent out an open invitation to acquaintances and those she felt she could trust, encouraging them to bring friends. She was sure to include those who could be counted on to gossip. Wagging tongues would do half the work for her, spreading the word about the delectable treats that were Eve Taylor's calling card.

She'd been prepping and buying for the last two days and was down to the wire. Baking, basting, and primping of goodies would take over her afternoon, but this morning was decoration time, and the troops were on their way.

In other words, Gabrielle and Joni.

Eve still had moments when she doubted the plan, and her own sanity, but forced herself to imagine a life of fear and hiding, never able to climb out of the shadows, unable to wring every last drop out of the life that awaited her. *Forget that.*

It was similar to an exercise regimen, only she was working out a mental muscle. If she'd gotten this far and was still pushing through the pain and doubt, it would be a terrible waste to just give up.

She peered out the window toward Trey's house and pictured his black hair and sensually dark eyes. There was something else she wasn't ready to give up on.

He'd only left her alone in the last week if she were with someone else or if her cell phone was securely attached to her body. This small allowance was during daylight hours and only if he were in close proximity. It had taken some female persistence to convince Trey the cell phone idea was valid, and Eve still caught him looking out his window at times to scout for enemies.

Like he was doing now. She met his gaze from the second story bathroom where he'd probably been showering. She gave him a two-finger salute and an impish smile. It was kind of a turn on, the way he was always checking up on her.

He still spent every night on her couch, or she stayed in his guest bedroom. She'd offered him the spare room at her place, but he said he wanted to be on the first floor. The implication of that still unnerved her, but operation live-free-or-die, literally, was still in effect. She wasn't giving up.

She heard the thumping from a block away, but it wasn't until the car pulled into her driveway that Eve could make out the distinctive sound of the Black Eyed Peas. Gabrielle was eclectic in all things.

She and Joni bumbled into the house, arms loaded down with bags of various creepy implements. "Where do you want all of this?" Gabrielle asked from somewhere beneath a huge black spider that seemed to be eating her.

"In the living room. There's more floor space there so we can designate it as headquarters," Eve said, taking some things from her Gypsy friend before they were dropped.

"Goblin central, huh?" Joni strolled in with considerably fewer items. "I like it." She dusted her hands together as if she'd lugged a stone from Giza's pyramids. "Why don't we call hunk-o-mighty over from next door. I wouldn't mind watching him flex those muscles." She wiggled her eyebrows and her glasses along with them.

"No, no. We can handle it." Eve wouldn't mind watching

Trey flex either, but she had a long to-do list, and he would only distract her. She found her mind wandering in that direction more and more, it seemed. It was becoming difficult to fall asleep knowing his bare chest was sleeping downstairs most nights.

Her steamy dreams about him were no escape either. She recalled the intensity of deep brown eyes under slashing brows, his chiseled face closing in as he lowered himself to lie on top of her in some unidentified room filled with a red glow and hot, swirling mists.

No need to pull out the symbolism book for that one.

"Well, come on then," Gabrielle said before heaving a sigh as if already utterly exhausted. "There's more to be unloaded."

"All in good taste I hope." Eve trailed her friend with a frown. "You stuck to the list, right? I have most of what I need, and I want it to be fun but tasteful."

"Do I ever do it any other way?"

Eve bit her tongue and grinned at the flamboyant turquoise shirt her friend was wearing with matching jeweled flats. "No, but you have a tendency to add your own...shall we say, flair?"

Now Gabrielle faked a pout. "I stuck to your stodgy old list." The pout rolled into a wicked leer. "Except for this one thing." She pulled out a crystal ball and a banner strung with shiny strands of beads. It read, *Madame Lola-Fortune Teller*. "I was envisioning the powder room in the upstairs hallway?"

"I wish I'd thought of it myself." Eve popped a kiss to Gabrielle's cheek.

Joni shook her head at the two older females hugging and laughing. "I didn't sign on for all that," she said and scooted inside. It wasn't long before Eve and Gabrielle heard a shriek of dismay followed by, "You have got to be kidding."

"What's that all about?" Gabrielle asked.

"My best guess," Eve said after grabbing the last of the items from Gabrielle's trunk, "is that she's just seen the pumpkins."

There were twenty in all, not including the smaller ones

mixed in with gourds. All were waiting to be emptied out for carving or etching.

"Holy Hannah," Gabrielle gasped when she edged up beside Joni to see what all the fuss was about. "Where was my gray matter when I suggested you have a party, Eve? I should have known what I was getting into."

"Yes, you should have, but now you're in it up to your knees. Don't worry, with the three of us, it will fly by."

Her two guests both gave her a look that clearly said they weren't buying it.

"I've spread a tarp out back with big plastic bowls for the guts."

At the word "guts," Joni's eyes lit up. "This is beginning to sound good after all. Where's my knife?"

Sometimes the girl was downright scary.

Eve pointed the way, and they all fell into cutting and scooping. It was busy work and messy work, but most surprising to Eve, it was fun. Occasionally she stopped to give herself a mental shake, still shocked to be immersing herself in the holiday she had boycotted for years. She hadn't carved a pumpkin since the afternoon of the abductions. Now here she was, covered up to her elbows in orange gunk.

Patterns for Jack-o'-lantern faces, witches, monsters, and leaves were used for the designs, with a little artistic license on each of their parts. It was mid-morning by the time everything was cleaned up to leave a population of orange faces littering the lawn.

"Cool. I feel like the Goblin King," Joni crooned as she did a pirouette. "Behold my minions."

"I think we need food. Somebody's sugar must be low," Gabrielle said with a smirk toward her one-of-a-kind employee. Then to Eve, "Nah. What am I saying? She's always like this."

"Ah ha ha!" Joni laughed in an imitation of Vincent Price, arms spread wide and swooping toward them like a vamp.

Eve ducked and laughed. "Sandwiches are in the fridge with

the drinks."

After a quick break, they set up tables in every available space, then covered them with white gauze, ragged at the edges, which was then overlain with black silk, cut in jagged points. The spider was hung in the foyer, ready to pounce on unsuspecting guests as they entered.

The pumpkins were strategically spread to each room and filled with candles. Eve knew that strands of lighting could be used to light them, but she preferred the flickering flames. It just seemed more authentic.

With everything in place except the food, Joni and Gabrielle helped Eve straighten up and toss the garbage before getting ready to go home and dress themselves. It wasn't a proper Halloween party if people didn't dress up. "Is there anything else we can do?" Gabrielle asked.

"No, I've got it from here. I'm going to get started on some of the more involved dishes then take a bath to reinvigorate," Eve said, stretching her arms above her head. Two hours bent over and carving had done a number on her back.

Gabrielle did a little jig. "I can't wait to set up my booth. I'll be back early to give you a hand with the final touches."

"Don't forget the candles."

Eve had requested a box of the gold-trimmed candles Gabrielle carried in her store. They would add a touch of the mystical as well as more of the dancing shadows that always followed flame. Eve would be lucky if she didn't burn the place down before the night was over.

She wondered what Trey would wear. He'd balked at the idea of wearing a costume, but Eve had insisted he couldn't show up without one. She doubted whatever he wore would be enough to dampen the lust that always reared up to clench her belly when she saw him.

They had barely touched since the night he'd found her out back. The night she'd told him all about her vivid imagination, for lack of a better word. She didn't think he was holding back because of that. It hadn't seemed to bother him in the least.

She imagined it was a matter of pride. Trey's code of honor would ensure he didn't take advantage of a woman in her situation. He would consider it unethical to sexually pursue a woman he was, due to his own insistence, protecting. It would be immoral.

Eve, on the other hand, was ready for a little immoral behavior.

Thinking of what she would be wearing tonight, Eve notched her chin up a degree, issuing a challenge her poor opponent didn't even know about. And he wouldn't until he was on his knees in defeat.

Boosted by the thought, Eve readied herself for more toil and trouble and imagined she would have just enough time for a manicure. She wiggled her fingers to appreciate the length of her nails and how good they would look once painted to match her outfit.

Oh, yeah. Trey's definitely going down, she purred to herself. She'd never known a man that could resist red.

~~~

Trey came in the front, not his usual back door entry, to get the full effect of the women's work. He didn't know how they'd gotten so much accomplished in one day, and he imagined Eve had been making every dish known to man in addition to decorating.

Black faux trees stood in the grass with gnarled, reaching branches. Small dots of red blinked from the lights wrapped around them. The wicked trees seemed alive with watchful eyes, and a coffin with its lid partially open lay between them, tempting the curious to peek in.

A witch leaned around the trunk of a real tree. She had lime hair and clawed fingers, the sort to cook children, and Trey wondered about the glowing pot at her feet. He moved closer to look inside only to jump back when the leering hag raised an arm and cackled. He wouldn't tell anyone he'd fallen for that, but imagined the scare others would have as the night wore on.

He was early, to offer a hand, even though he'd been warned to wait until party-time, and to be costumed up or else. He wore black from head to toe, military boots completing the ensemble, and a belt at his waist holstering strange implements. Holy water, a stake, and a small propane torch. The large silver cross around his neck completed the outfit of a modern day Van Helsing. The modern was his refusal to wear the swirling cape and ruffled shirt. He would only go so far, even for Eve.

He held Max under one arm. The golden puppy was dressed in a toddler-sized black T-shirt with the neck and arms cut out to fit. Trey had created a design on his computer and printed it on clear adhesive to stick to the fabric. The words across Max's back proudly told the world he was a "Vamp Hunter."

Passing small totems of pumpkin and gourd faces, Trey walked in without knocking and entered a world that any black-hearted, fright night loving American would appreciate. He let the puppy loose and refrained from cringing at the spider over his head then made his way toward the kitchen.

Moving about the room like flaming glory, Eve wore her hair piled atop her head with cascading ringlets. He had no idea what type of dress she wore with short sleeves puffed at the shoulders and a high tight waist, but he couldn't complain. The rich murder red fabric fell straight to the floor.

He thought he liked her snug jeans the best, but the feminine elegance of the dress and the way it hugged her curves caused an instant reaction. He'd never desired her more than he did now and wanted to run his hand under those silk layers and up a long, golden thigh.

She turned around and gave him a view of the barest of cleavage, just enough to make a man want more, then smiled as if reading his lustful mind. "And what are you supposed to be?" she asked, eyes roving over his black-clad body in a way that hardened him and made him wish he could turn the clock forward and have the house empty but for the two of them.

He noticed two red spots angled on her neck that wept streaks of blood. "Looks like I'm your adversary tonight. If that bite has turned you."

A dangerous and sexual sound purred deep in her throat. "Come closer and find out."

Trey had never considered role-playing or understood the peculiar fetish. But he was beginning to.

"I'll have to drop my belt before you can get any closer," he tossed back.

Eve's eyes grew hooded then regretful. "Pity I have guests coming. That sounded like a dare."

Recognizing hazardous ground, Trey backtracked. "I'm surprised you wore that. I thought you didn't like anything scary."

"I don't like Halloween. I never said I couldn't appreciate certain aspects of folklore and superstition. Besides, something about being immortal for one night appealed to me." She tilted her head to a black cauldron sitting on the island between them. "Mind carrying that to the table in the parlor? The green one."

"Green table?" he asked, lifting the witch's bowl to find a slime-green liquid with floating eyeballs.

"You'll know it when you see it."

"Think anyone will drink this stuff?"

"Absolutely. It's lemon-lime punch, my own concoction. So good it will make your eyes pop out." She smirked at her own joke before Trey left, shaking his head.

For someone who didn't like Halloween, Eve had gone all out. He passed a black and white draped table in the den with another cauldron, this one filled with punch the color of cherries and also swimming with eyeballs. A variety of cookies were arranged for display as well as a few cakes, one with a spider web design of chocolate piping. Everything there had an orange or red hue. Theme tables, both in color and content.

In the parlor he saw more cobwebs clinging to every corner or doorway. It worried him a little, given the number of candles weaving bright flames in each room. There was a table of cheese, some veined with blue, others a deep emerald, bottles of cucumbers and what looked like white carrots. There were black and green olives, dips, white crackers, and an open spot where he placed the punch bowl. She had been right. It was a green table.

A sparkly skeleton whose bones had evidently rotted and been filled with glitter, sat in a chair to observe any who partook of the food. With a grin for the foolishness of it all, Trey passed through the foyer to glimpse Gabrielle sashaying down the steps. She was a Gypsy through and through in a mass of colorful skirts, white pleasant blouse, and lace-up vest of saffron yellow. A purple bandana fought to contain her wild brown waves of hair while large golden hoops dangled from her ears.

"Hey, I thought you were supposed to wear a costume," Trey teased, knowing full well she would take it in stride.

She did, and shot him a ring-fingered bird before putting on a thick accent. "Would the warrior like to have his fortune told? What will it be, riches, fame, or love?"

He frowned and cocked his head. "Maybe later, Esmerelda. I'm assisting the vamp queen at the moment."

"Got you in her thrall, has she?"

More than you know.

Feeling uncomfortable with the turn of his thoughts and the knowing look in Gabrielle's eyes, Trey continued down the hallway. He noticed more tables covered in pasta dishes and pastries filled with meat or fruit. People would eat well here tonight, and Eve would have the reputation she deserved.

He had to hand it to Gabrielle. This had been a stroke of genius.

He came through the side door to see Eve standing with

hands on hips and surveying her culinary kingdom. "I think everything is in place," she said to herself and Trey, turning to face him. "What do you think?"

"Terrifying and appetizing."

"Then the goal is met," she said, surprising him by coming to him and wrapping her arms around his neck, waiting for him to take what was offered.

Trey bent his head to hers and felt the depth of her longing. The gentle, trembling kiss told him more than anything Eve could have said. Her lust for him was his undoing, and fierce possessiveness came over him, a great hand of need that clutched and wouldn't let go. Despite his defensiveness and maneuvers, he'd fallen after all.

They pulled apart at the sound of the doorbell. It had been changed to belt an ominous chorus of dongs with terrified human cries in the background. The woman had thought of everything.

Eve wiped his mouth, he assumed to remove lipstick, then backed away to check her own lips in the window's reflection. "Okay," she said with a spin and swirl of crimson. "Show time."

FIFTEEN

The turnout was greater than any of them had hoped for or expected. Eve's home was packed with people. Many were there because they knew Gabrielle or Lance, but others came for the food or to see inside the historic old house. Some just came for the party and a chance to dress up. It never ceased to amaze Eve how popular Halloween was.

Though she wasn't thrilled the dreaded holiday was drawing closer, some of the nauseating fear had abated. She was doing her best to face this one on her own terms. To put her stamp on it instead of feeling the burning brand left on every previous Halloween. The stench of death and brutality had always persisted, roused by the sight of candy corn and pumpkins.

The kidnapper had stolen her away from a celebration of ghosts and goblins then introduced her to an entirely different sort of demon.

Eve had left her purity, naiveté, and a great chunk of her ability to trust in that basement, to emerge as only a fragile shell of the impetuous girl she'd been before. Time and loved ones had helped her build a life, but there had always been missing pieces. There were holes that couldn't be filled, because stubborn stains of evil resided there.

Eve finally felt those gouges healing now, ever so slightly, but that small amount of change at this late date gave her something she thought never to feel again. Hope.

Hope that she might have a normal life with a man who knew all about the nightmares that stalked her in the light as easily as the dark. About visions that could cripple her at any given hour. A man who understood why she trembled at the sight of a fall carnival.

A man who would love her still.

Jarred by a tap on her shoulder, Eve turned to find Joni and Thomas standing together. Joni sported a pale blue shirt that read *Metallica*, while Thomas wore a gray one in support of the band *AC-DC*. "Skulls are cool. Uhhh-uh," Thomas said before emitting an odd chuckle that sounded almost painful.

"Shut-up, Butthead." Joni elbowed her friend, and spoke in a drawl that sounded straight from a California surfing convention.

"You two nailed it. I can say that much," Eve said, giving them mock applause for the performance.

"Beavis and Butthead. From your generation, right?" Joni asked.

Eve rolled her eyes. "Um, not quite."

"Anyway, it's classic." Thomas shrugged. "Need some help?"

"Nope. You two are off duty, so just hang out and have a good time." She reconsidered and gave them a wink. "You can help by making noises of ecstasy when you eat something. Help sell the natives on my brilliance."

"No problem there." Thomas rubbed his stomach in anticipation.

In the living room near the fireplace Eve saw an unexpected sight. She'd invited Nan's lawyer, Kurt Dennis, but was surprised he'd shown. Adding to the oddity of the situation was what he wore. His usual uniform of expensively tailored suits had been replaced by a plain white T-shirt and khaki pants, making him look familiar somehow.

"Kurt," she said in greeting. "Good to see you here."

He set his cup of lime punch on the mantle next to a trio of antique style bottles labeled *Arsenic, Poison*, and *Devil Tonic*. When he crossed his arms across his chest and smiled brightly, the mystery solved itself.

Eve recognized the posture. "Or should I call you Mr. Clean?"

Rubbing the smoothness of his scalp, Kurt grinned. "I was halfway there already."

His cheerful manner was out of character, and he seemed relaxed. Eve noted again the muscles rippling in his arms. It appeared the attorney spent some hours in the gym.

"You know Sam," he stated.

She took in the man beside him in jeans and light blue shirt, a bolo around his neck as the only hint of what he was supposed to be. "Trey's friend? No, we haven't met, though I'm grateful for your skill with cars." Eve extended her hand. "You saved my life."

After an uncertain pause, Sam took it and shook firmly before pulling back. Dirty blonde hair was cut short with a few spiky bangs over his forehead. The mix of boy-next-door good looks and outdoorsman confidence probably drove the ladies mad, but now he offered a shy grin that made Eve think he might be mildly embarrassed.

He covered it with a put-on of, "Shucks, ma'am. Think nothing of it."

Eve laughed good-naturedly. "The van is wonderful workmanship, so thank you."

With the awkward moment passed, Eve asked if they'd sampled the rigatoni with roasted tomatoes. "It looks simple, but I promise you won't forget it.

"Working my way from room to room," Kurt said before Eve left them to resume talk of football, fishing, or whatever male topic they'd been so engrossed in before her arrival.

She wanted to make sure she spoke with everyone, as a proper hostess should. Even if she was a walking version of the undead.

A skitter and thump followed by several female coos told Eve that Max was serving as one of the main attractions. She rounded the corner to the kitchen, hoping the puppy wasn't wetting on any of the guests.

Though Trey still dodged any admission of dog-love, he and Max had become inseparable. They both stuck to Eve like burrs, so the three of them were usually together. Like a little family.

The idea rippled across Eve's heart with a warm, soothing feeling. She'd given Trey the puppy to encourage him to form an attachment, if only to a pet, but the plan had worked on her instead. She was the one falling in love. With the dog and his man.

She made her way through the throngs of devils, witches, and television characters intent on locating her vampire killer. She'd last seen Trey exiting out the back and decided to push the boundary just a little bit more. *Maybe he'll let me hold his stake.*

Clenching her eyes at her own corny and tawdry joke, Eve lifted her skirts and floated down the back steps like a queen. Here she had set up seating areas with her own outdoor furniture and any she could plead, borrow, or buy cheap. Tables were draped in dark gray muslin to create uniformity. They all had candles burning in scarlet glass containers that shone like rubies in the night.

Farther out and to the left was a bonfire. That duty she had gladly handed over to Trey, and now she saw silhouettes of people standing and talking around the flames. The mood was lively and fun, with the thrill of dark magic in the air that came from embracing the more sinister side of humanity. The side that appreciated a bump in the night and the accompanying rush of adrenaline. The night might make people wonder what really waited for them in the obsidian forest at the edge of Eve's lawn. That was part of the thrill.

Eve looked proudly out over the faux graveyard beyond the seating areas. There were headstones of different sizes with a few tilted to appear aged and partially swallowed by the earth. Of course, no dead bodies rested in her back yard, but the fake cemetery was a nice touch. Gargoyles guarded the entry path, and a well-placed fog machine and blue yard lights made the area seem treacherous and unholy.

I can't believe I'm actually enjoying myself. Eve recalled the boys playing around her neighbors' decorative gravestone and the chill she'd gotten. Now she stood marveling at the thoroughly gruesome fun land she had created in her own home.

Those holes inside her stitched themselves together just a bit more.

She remembered her reason for coming outside and searched the crowd for Trey. His full black ensemble wouldn't stick out amongst all the other gloomy costumes.

But the lacy pink skirt and blonde bob of hair did. Especially given the fact that Mandy Pickerson, owner of said bob and skirt, currently had a hand on Trey's arm and was leaning toward him in an all female and all too provocative way. Tinkerbell was doing her best to advertise her wares, and Eve, the vampire queen, considered walking up to take a bite of the perky fairy.

Eve slid up next to Trey and raised one brow before offering a dagger of a smile to Mandy. "I'm more than shocked to see you here. Can't believe you would have the guts."

Mandy pointed a cotton-candy fingernail in the direction of a man Eve didn't recognize. "He invited me. I understood this party was open to whoever wanted to come." She tossed her hair and repositioned a bag on her arm. A small furry head with a pink bow peeked out of the matching purse and sniffed.

Ignoring the poor thing, Eve spoke with a chill in her normally warm voice. "It is, but I didn't think you would have the poor taste to come to my home after your last scam. Angling for another sensationalism?"

Mandy blinked like a coquette. "I can't help what sells, Eve. I just do my job." And her eyes turned to mischief. "Trey and I were only catching up. It's been too long since we spent any time together." She sent a sidelong smile to Trey that told Eve all she needed or wanted to know.

With her malicious deed done for the day, Mandy waltzed away to join a group by the bonfire. Eve and Trey both remained silent. One in distaste, the other unsure what to say.

Trey finally decided to cut the heart out. "We dated once or twice. Never had sex."

Unappeased, Eve ground out, "Well, which was it? Once or twice?"

"Twice."

"Hmph." Eve sighed and looked over his shoulder into the fire."I wish you'd mentioned it, considering the article and how I feel about it. And her."

Lifting his cross and leaning back as if in fear for his life, Trey begged, "Please don't bite me."

Unable to stay angry for no real reason, Eve pouted her lips. "I can't promise anything."

His arm was around her waist in a second, his fingers kneading the flesh of her hip, chest pressed to chest. "Then you'll understand if I bite back." He lowered his mouth to place a kiss on her shoulder.

It was simple and chaste, but the light touch inflamed Eve's blood so the crisp wind no longer cooled her skin. Parts of her pulsed wildly and woke with a vicious hunger.

"When is this party going to be over?" Trey murmured against her ear in a voice so graveled Eve knew he was starving the same way she was.

"Not soon enough." Recalling they were surrounded by others, Eve stepped back and held his hand out as if they'd just concluded a dance. Which, in a primitive way, they had.

"I should go back in. Check to see what needs refilling," she said with a spring in her step and a promise in her eyes.

Getting back inside took longer than anticipated, since many of the guests stopped Eve to compliment the food or house, or to extend their welcome back to Pine Creek. She felt more and more at ease with each gracious gesture and was full of joy from the turnout of friends as well as the party's success.

"Hey, sorry I wasn't here earlier," Lance said as he rushed to her side from out of nowhere. He looked hurried and flushed, giving Eve a good idea why her brother was late.

"Did you bring her with you?"

"Who?" he asked before waving to someone behind her.

Eve didn't respond. She let her silence do the questioning.

"No, I didn't. Couldn't find a costume in time." Lance frowned, put out that his sister could read him so well.

"You've known about the party for a week."

Now the sinful smile was back on his face. "Yeah, but I've only known *her* for a few hours." He kissed Eve's cheek and made his escape before she could chastise him.

Rain and spring. Chocolate and peanut butter. Lance and women. Some things just naturally went together.

Mandy's dog started yipping somewhere farther out, bringing a fully-wired Max scrambling down the steps in search of a possible playmate. The barking grew closer as the pink-bowed dog bounced across the yard. Mandy gave chase as fast as she could in stilettos. "Suki! Come here! You'll get your paws dirty!"

The two dogs met face to face and Max pulled up short as if unsure what kind of creature Suki actually was. Taking after her mother, Suki promptly curved around Max to check out his hind quarters and give him a good sniffing.

Max returned the favor, so the two moved slowly in an odd canine-fairy-vamp-hunter circle.

"Ooh. Stop that." Mandy picked up her dog and wiped its paws with a nearby cocktail napkin before putting her safely back in the bag. Suki looked disappointed, while Mandy glared at Eve.

It was too comical, and Eve couldn't contain the laugh when Lance stepped up to whisper, "Way to go, Max. A dog after my own heart."

"Cut it out," Eve said with a smile before slapping him on the arm.

Mandy walked away in a huff and was lost again in the crowd.

Above in the black sky, the moon eased itself slowly as hours passed and the festivity waned. Only stragglers remained by midnight, and many grabbed something to snack on as they exited. That was the greatest compliment as far as Eve was concerned.

She'd made enough food for a Roman army, but several things ran out anyway, and nothing was left of the backup supply. She wouldn't have that much leftover, and her heart did a happy jig.

Gabrielle, Joni, Thomas, and Trey were already straightening up, even though she had told them repeatedly to let her do it. She didn't want to seem like she was hurrying the last guests out.

"We'll be discreet," Gabrielle had reassured her. "Just the empties, and I promise we won't wash a thing."

Lance had already gone, with Eve's assurance that he was excused. She had a sneaking suspicion he was on his way back to the entertaining female he'd pulled himself away from, or off of, to attend the party in the first place.

"Hey, Eve," Thomas called out. "Someone left you a card."

Blood drained from her head as she searched for Thomas. He came from the living room and into the hallway where she stood saying goodnight to a golf buddy of her father's. He and his wife had mentioned their upcoming anniversary and their need for a caterer.

The bubble of delight from their request burst when Eve saw the orange envelope in Thomas's hand. The world shifted into slow motion as he came closer step by step, holding it out to her.

The roar in her ears stopped suddenly with a pop when he said, "It was under one of the trays when I picked it up." He continued to offer it, but his features furrowed in confusion when Eve didn't take the note from him. "It has your name on it."

Somehow Trey materialized beside her, grabbing the repulsive thing from Thomas, causing the younger man to ease back. "What's the matter? Was it a surprise?" He apparently thought he'd spoiled a secret letter from Trey.

"It's fine," Trey told him. "You didn't do anything wrong."

Thomas looked again to Eve, and the worry in his eyes told her she was as pale as she felt. "It's okay, you just surprised me."

"I'm sorry, really."

Feeling terrible for causing him so much distress, Eve tried to cover a big lie with a smaller version of it. "I've had a secret admirer of sorts, and he just won't take no for an answer." She glanced at Trey. "I was worried about Trey seeing it and getting upset."

Picking up on the ruse, Trey said, "And I was worried about you, so I guess we both overreacted. Sorry, Thomas."

Managing a smile, Eve put a hand on the young man's shoulder. "Me, too."

"Good. I mean...not so good, but better than what I thought. You looked like you were going to faint." Thomas heaved a breath and visibly relaxed. "You really freaked me out."

He started to walk away, then stopped and drew his lip to the side in thought. "Man, I can't believe this guy had the *cojones* to come to your party."

Eve and Trey looked at each other as their romantic plans melted away, and she was sure they were thinking the same thing.

Neither can I.

Sixteen

I am blessed with dear friends, Eve thought as she took in her clean and organized home. She had assumed Gabrielle, Joni, and Thomas left the night before when she and Trey had, but they'd evidently stayed and cleaned up, leaving only the decorations out for Eve. She now had more Halloween-themed items than she knew what to do with. Luckily, the house had a huge attic.

The props had been a good investment, and the party had been a smash. Eve had come away with one new job and the possibility of more. Everything had gone according to plan, just the way she liked it.

Until her stalker made his way into her home to leave his last little offering.

Eve and Trey had relocated to his house at his insistence. With no fight or energy left in her, Eve had gone straight to Trey's bed. And Trey had gone straight to his guns.

Having gotten little sleep, Eve was still deflated and didn't want to deal with the poem. She'd insisted they leave it unopened until today, and was more than happy to continue to procrastinate. She dreaded finding out what the killer had to say. Looking around at the decorations, Eve decided to make a few changes to take her mind off creepy letters and murder.

The glittery green skeleton soon found a new home on the front porch in a rocking chair. The better to welcome trick-or-treaters. She took down the large spider in the foyer, because it was a little too real and managed to startle her every time she walked in. The graveyard would stay put. It was awesome and could be seen from the street, so it would serve until the big night.

The big night. Halloween. *This is without a doubt the longest month of my life.*

Firing up her drug of choice, the coffee pot, Eve rested against the counter and followed Trey's every move with her eyes. He was taking care of the borrowed tables and chairs that needed to be returned to their owners.

He was so much more than her neighbor now and more than just a sexual interest, especially since they hadn't managed to score that touchdown yet. Somehow he had become a fixture in her life. They were essentially a couple, having fallen into a routine that needed no justification. Nothing to clarify. They simply were.

Eve was content to leave it that way. She didn't ask anymore about his plans for the future, because she wasn't sure she wanted to know. She had chosen to live her life to the fullest, and that was still her intent. No promises. No regrets.

Her phone sang out, and she answered with no real interest in talking to anyone. Her mind was occupied with enough for now.

It was Miranda, the woman who'd asked Eve to cater her son's birthday party. She and her husband had also come to Eve's last night. They made polite conversation and chuckled over some of the events at the Halloween party before Miranda's voice changed, and Eve realized there was more to her call.

"Eve, I think you're brilliant and talented. Your cooking is phenomenal, the ideas are fresh…"

Eve heard the hesitation. "But?"

"With what's happening, I just can't take the risk of having you do the birthday party. I'm so sorry. It's too dangerous, and I have to think of my child."

"What do you mean?" Eve clenched the phone in her hand.

"The newspaper article out today. It's all about your notes

and that you're being followed and threatened. Didn't you see it?" Miranda sounded surprised, with a touch of fear.

Eve was no longer concerned about the party or dragging out explanations. She had to read that article. *Damn Mandy. What have you done?* "I understand, Miranda. I really do, and thanks for letting me know so quickly."

She dropped the phone and dashed out to look for the paper, finding it in its usual place. The shrubbery. She didn't hesitate like the last time The Herald brought unpleasant news, but she wrenched it from between the leaves, tearing off the plastic wrapper with a vengeance. Better to take the violence out on the paper than on Mandy.

Trey was in the kitchen helping himself to the coffee by holding a mug under the stream. "I couldn't wait, and it's about finished..." He noticed her fluster. "What's happened? Now," he added.

Eve held up The Herald and shook it in her tightened fingers as if that alone was answer enough.

And it was. "Our favorite reporter's been at it again?" Trey continued to mix milk in his drink without apparent concern.

"You mean our favorite fiction writer, because that's what half of it usually is." Eve was steamed. "Two sweeteners and fat free creamer please."

Trey readied the second cup. "I know your routine by now."

"Oh, you do, huh? Then what's my next move?"

"By the look in your eye, I'd say Mandy should stay tucked under her rock for the day."

"Got that right." Eve braced herself on the counter, still not bothering to open the paper fully. "I'm going to go talk to her."

"No." Trey took another drink, still the picture of composure, which made Eve feel even more unraveled.

"Yes, I am."

He finally moved, leaning on the opposite side of the island to meet her stare to stubborn stare. "We have bigger things to see to, and you haven't even read the article yet."

"Well, I will now." Eve stomped to the corner nook and sat with a thump, spreading the pages and reading silently for a couple of minutes before letting loose a sound that was half-scream, half-growl. "She has absolutely no professional ethics." Eve tapped the paper with her fingertip. "And her grammar stinks."

"While you're still calm," Trey said with more than a little sarcasm, "why don't we handle the other thing. You know, the one that might actually require police intervention?"

Knowing he referred to the letter, Eve threw up her hands. "They didn't think it was serious before. Why would this time be any different?'

Sitting beside her and bumping her farther into the seating with his hip, Trey rubbed her leg. "Why don't we see what we have to work with before making any assumptions?"

His touch and the fact he had brought her coffee in her favorite cup helped tame the wild fury Eve had been riding. She let her head rest on his shoulder and closed her eyes. "I can't believe you're still here with me, after all this." She blew out a sigh. "I can't believe I'm still here after all this."

He cupped her face in his palm then simply placed the poem from last night in front of her. "Then let's get through it once and for all, so we can see where we stand without murder and worry between us. I'd like to know what we could do on our own."

Eve raised her eyes to him in disbelief. This was the first time he'd ever referred to their having a real relationship. One that was worth making stronger. Because that implied a future.

"Yes. Let's do that," she whispered before taking the envelope gently by the corner, as Trey had been handling it, just in case there was a need for fingerprinting. They both expected the police to show the same level of disinterest, but carelessness would help no one.

In silence, she slipped a knife under the small tack of

adhesive and let the orange paper fall from its sheath. Using the point of the blade and the tip of one finger to hold it open, Eve read the lines to herself as Trey did the same.

The girl who never heard she couldn't do something
Should watch out 'cause here I come
And I'm bound to teach you more than one thing

"Hmph," Eve said after a moment. "This one's different."

"Right, it addresses three different people," Trey said, nodding.

Eve looked back over the words. "I meant it was more threatening, but I see what you mean. He mentions the girl, himself, and then speaks to me."

"Definitely two entities, you and another woman." Trey reached for the laptop that was always close at hand. "Does it bring anything to mind?"

"No. Nothing." Eve watched as he typed in words from the poem in the search bar, having no luck with the first few tries. "Try one full sentence. The first one."

The ray of light that had been lancing across the table disappeared, causing Eve to glance up at the sky through the windows surrounding the nook where they sat. Dreary gray clouds were rolling over the sun, blotting out the radiance of morning. A streak of something like black lighting shot through her chest, even before she turned to see what Trey had found.

"Here," he said. "It's part of a song."

Locking her eyes to the computer screen, Eve felt her pupils dilate and her veins ice over. Her heart thundered in her head. "Oh, God. It can't be."

Trey jerked around to her, grabbing her hand and shoulder. "Eve, what is it? Stay with me now. I need you."

Eve could feel the iron of his grip, the unwavering strength of him as he tried to channel it into her. *He's afraid I'm going under*, she thought. The realization was enough to clamp down on the nightmare knocking at her mind like a ghoul begging to be invited in.

"I'm okay. I'm okay." She took a drink of coffee to prove it, but shock drew her hand to the computer again where she pointed an accusing finger. "I was right. I didn't know it. I thought I was crazy. Paranoid. But I was right."

"Right about what?"

"One of them was Snow White," she said then tapped the same finger on the monitor that displayed the lyrics to a theme song. "And one of them was Pippi Longstocking."

She looked to Trey, still unable to fully comprehend for herself what she was about to tell him. Or why it was happening. "It's him. He's back."

She shut her eyes. "And he's killing them all over again."

~~~

After Eve's revelation, Trey decided they would go to the police this time and make sure they understood the connection. And that Eve was in real danger. He also hoped to sway them by pointing out that she was their one real witness. Eve was the only person who could identify the man who'd taken her and the other children to his basement of horrors. She was the only survivor.

It was a half-hour drive to the neighboring town of Verde Hill. It was home to the local college and large enough to have a fully functioning homicide detail. The rolling hills they passed were soft with the colors of autumn, and Trey understood why so many "tree-peepers" flocked to this part of the state to watch the leaves fade from green to a rainbow of ambers and reds. Rarely was death such a beautiful sight.

Trey and Eve were both silent for the ride, lost in their own thoughts. As he glanced at her nervously picking her fingernails, the urge to shield her from the dirty business ahead rose up in him again.

He'd meant what he said to her earlier, about wanting to see what they could have if left alone with the peace and sanctity of a normal life. The constant need to guard her from danger made it hard to decipher the source of his feelings. He'd been a soldier. Protecting those in peril was second nature, regardless of any personal intimacy.

Then there was the guilt. He had promised to watch her and report back to Kurt Dennis as Nan had requested. The lie that had been a small crack in the road was now a massive rift, one that might swallow any hope of a future with Eve. That was the problem with deception.

After everything they'd been dealing with and all Eve had shared, his omission of such a vital piece of information would be a blow to their relationship. Which is why he had to figure out just what the hell she meant to him. If he wanted to salvage anything when the threat was over, he would have to tell her.

If his need for a solitary life won in the end, then she never had to know.

Finally pulling up to the police station, they climbed out of their respective sides of Trey's car, but when they entered the building, Eve latched onto his hand. Her fingers were cold despite having been in the heat for so long, and Trey held on, needing the contact as much as she did.

He had called ahead, using the number Detective Curtis had written on the back of the card he'd given Eve. He and his partner would be waiting, having been told there might be a connection between Eve's stalker and the murders.

The station looked as one might expect it to with white tiled floor and gray walls. When they exited the elevator on the second floor, the environment changed to a more pleasing decor. The walls were painted sage green, and the floor was softened by carpet of a dark gray composite. Someone must have thought the hard-working police force needed a soothing atmosphere.

The ever-so-slick Detective Reston walked up to them. "This

way," he said with an open-handed gesture for them to proceed down the hall. "Last door on the left. Can I bring anything to drink?"

"No, thanks," Eve and Trey said in unison, and for some reason, it drew a smile from Eve.

They found Detective Curtis waiting for them with an open folder on his desk and papers in tidy piles. He stood and motioned to the two chairs facing his desk, then sat opposite of them. "So, tell me what new information you have and why you feel the person harassing you is the same one committing these murders."

Trey held back, letting Eve take the lead.

"Each of the poems I've gotten have been riddles as well as poems, giving us hints to certain people or, as we've discovered, characters." Eve sat forward and brought the letters out of her purse to lay in front of the detective. They were in a plastic bag now, to prevent any more contamination than they'd already received. Thankfully, Eve hadn't wanted to handle them much.

"Characters?" Detective Curtis picked up some papers of his own to peruse, and Trey saw they were typed copies of the poems. The detective must have written them down in completion when he'd first interviewed Eve. "This first one. Who is it referring to then?"

"That one is Snow White." Eve tightened her hands on the arm of her chair and fell silent.

Trey took over. "The second is an allusion to a character called Cagliostro. We found out it was a short story about an evil magician, but today, we made a further discovery." He glanced at Eve and continued. "The short story was eventually re-adapted and re-written to become something more popular. It was the basis for the original movie, "The Mummy.""

Detective Curtis stared at Trey before he grimaced. "I'm afraid I understand, but go ahead and tell me the third." Detective Reston walked in, but Curtis held up a hand, causing his partner to lean quietly against the wall.

"Last night he left me another, and did so in the middle of a Halloween party I was having."

"At your house?" Reston asked, the bold move of the stalker surprising him as it had Eve and Trey.

"Yes." She answered him and looked back to the older man seated across from her. "The poem was about Pippi Longstocking."

Curtis nodded in acceptance. "Three of the children killed by the man who kidnapped you. They were dressed in those costumes."

"So there is a reason he's bringing these letters to you. But what does he expect to get out of it?" Reston asked Eve. "Some sort of thrill to be sharing it with you? Terrorizing you the way he does the other victims?"

"Or letting her know she's next," Trey said. "It follows that this is the same man from before, and he's recreating that night. The murders started when Eve came back to Pine Creek. He's sending the poems to Eve."

Trey took Eve's hand because he knew it was difficult for her to hear, and it was almost as difficult for him to say. "The only person who got away from him was Eve. He has unfinished business."

"He was never caught, and we don't have a name. The house he used had been abandoned, and a lucky break led us there. Someone reported smoke rising from the chimney, or we would never have found it," Curtis explained.

And they never would have found Eve alive. There was no need for him to state the obvious. They all understood.

"This man, he would be what, in his fifties now, right?" Reston asked. "You really think he's pulling this off?"

Curtis shrugged. "I don't know what to think, but you can be sure we'll look into this. You've just given us a lot more to work with." He focused hard on Eve. "It goes without saying, but if you see anything at all that tweaks your radar…"

"You'll be the first," Trey answered. He didn't mention that if he came face to face with the killer, the police would only need to bring a body bag. He wasn't going to let anything happen to Eve.

"We'll need a list of everyone at your party, and a short one of anyone you think might be capable of this. Anyone you've had disagreements with."

"The only two people I've had trouble with are Sturg Murray and Mandy Pickerson, but Sturg wasn't at the party and Mandy, well, I hate to be sexist, but she's a woman, and I just don't think whoever's responsible for all of this is female." Eve lifted a hand to take the notebook Curtis was offering, but noticed his distraction.

Trey saw it, too. Curtis had stopped mid-motion to catch his partner's eye before asking Eve, "Do you remember Ms. Pickerson leaving with anyone specific?"

"No, I don't." Eve looked at Trey with haunted eyes.

Trey shook his head. "I didn't see her leave, but she came with a date, so I assume the same man took her home. Why?"

Curtis let the pad of paper drop near Eve. "We'll still need that list, and we need to find out the name of who she was with." His mouth was tight and his eyes grim. "Mandy Pickerson's car was found abandoned on a road outside of town. It looks like a struggle occurred inside the vehicle."

"The same pattern," Eve gasped. "I got a note last night, and now Mandy..."

She let the words hang in the air, so Trey finished for her. "Now Mandy is missing."

Seventeen

Trey stoked the fire, encouraging the newly set logs to rest closer to the kindling now sputtering and sparking to life. There was plenty of wood stacked up next to the hearth, so they were set for the night. The central heating worked fine, but Eve needed comfort measures.

Crackling flames, beer for Trey, Chardonnay for her, and a thrown-together mix of party leftovers serving as dinner. Only one thing was missing in Eve's mind, and she planned to remedy that.

Spreading a couple of blankets over the large rug already softening the floor, she made a pallet with room for two. At Trey's questioning look, she explained, "Since you insist on sleeping down here, I'll just have to join you." She held his gaze so there would be no chance he misunderstood.

Judging by the heat in his eyes, he understood perfectly. "This is a bad time for you, Eve," he started with the usual argument.

"I know, I know. Your code of chivalry won't let you take advantage of the vulnerable maiden in her time of need." She stepped to him, placing her palm flat against his chest. They stood there a moment, eyes locked and hearts pounding for each other until Eve said on a low breath, "But there's only one thing I'm in need of."

Trey shook his head. "Let me rephrase. This is the worst time for you. Today you found out the man who stole you and changed your life forever is doing it all over again. That he's more than likely coming after you."

Eve put a finger to Trey's lips, but he took it gently in his hand. "Add to that you're feeling guilty about Mandy. And don't tell me you're not, because I know you," he said when she opened her mouth to disagree. "You and she had harsh words, so you regret that now."

She could only nod. He'd pegged her emotions exactly.

"And I know you think all of this is somehow your fault, that you're responsible for the new murders."

"Aren't I?" she asked, heat in her voice from the guilt he'd mentioned clawing its way into her throat. "My coming back is what triggered him to start again. Even if he's ultimately responsible, the fact remains that those people would still be alive if I'd refused the house and stayed where I was. My decisions, even if I couldn't have known, led to their deaths."

"No." Trey shook her lightly when she looked away, forcing her to see the truth in his words. "No, Eve. His decisions. His sickness. You are not responsible."

"It's just so hard." She left him to sit on the couch and pulled herself into a ball. "When I realized I had to move back to Pine Creek to save Nan's house, I knew it was going to take everything I had to hold it together. To keep from breaking apart. I would never have stayed if I'd known how things would go."

Trey kept his distance, standing in front of the fireplace. "I don't think that's true. You're stronger than you realize, and however bad all of this has been, you've stood up to it. You've found your courage when you had to." He softened his voice. "You will get through this, and he'll be caught."

Eve gave a short laugh of disbelief. "If I'm so strong, why are you afraid to touch me?" She took a deep breath and forced herself to ask the question she'd been avoiding. "Do you think I'm crazy? Is that why you always stop yourself and pull away from me? You talk about finding out what's between us, but you're still afraid of something."

"Unsure. Not afraid," he stated plainly. "I'm used to being in control of any situation I put myself in, and I thought I was with you."

"Now you're not?"

"I haven't felt in control since I kissed you on that damn ugly couch."

Eve smiled, and rubbed a hand over the floral print. If they did get though this, and he stayed, she might have to find a way to keep the old sofa after all.

She looked at him, standing there so steady and noble. He might laugh if he could read her mind and hear her think of him that way, but it was true. He had helped her every step of the way, protected her when she'd needed it, and held her up when she'd wavered.

The firelight deepened the shadows in the room, illuminating the strong features of the man she was falling in love with. His eyes seemed deeper, darker than normal, and they roamed Eve's body as she unfolded herself to stand slowly. Those brown eyes flickered to her hands in surprise when she started to unbutton her shirt.

Eve was going in for the kill, and the predatory man she had first met on a crisp autumn afternoon…he had become the hunted.

"Well, since you're not in control when you're with me, I guess that makes you the one who's vulnerable," she said with a purr, moving closer to him one sensual step at a time. "So I'm the one taking advantage."

"Eve," Trey growled as she stopped halfway down the buttons, spreading the neckline in invitation.

She didn't heed the warning in his voice, knowing the heat was due to arousal more than irritation. He wouldn't put up much of a fight, and she felt no qualms about pushing past his last reservations. She would stroke the passion between them until there was no room for rational thinking.

Eve stopped just within arm's reach. "I need your hands on

me." She met his eyes so he would see how much. "I need you."

The look he gave her started something like a gentle flow of lava in her belly. It began to shift and spread as he cupped the back of her head and brought her to meet him. How could a kiss be full of hesitation and liquid steel at the same time? And how was she supposed to remain standing when her legs wanted to wrap around him then and there?

A fiendish grin replaced the doubtful frown he'd worn moments before. "You can take all the advantage of me you want," he said, stroking the angle of her jaw, down to her neck and stopping just short of the valley between her breasts where his finger skimmed over the sensitive skin. "But you'll be doing it slowly."

Entranced, she allowed him to skim his hands down the center of her body and lazily undo the last few buttons before ridding her of the shirt. Those same slow hands grasped her back and held her against his broad chest while he teased and pressed before finally making his way to release her bra.

After a brief brush of his lips across her neck he asked, "You still sure about this?"

Now it was Eve's turn to set the pace, and she relayed her intentions by grasping his thick black hair. It was silky and cool between her fingers and she used her grip to bring his gaze to hers. "I'm not afraid of you," she said, nipping lightly at his bottom lip before suddenly diving in.

She wasn't afraid, not of giving herself to him. Not of this moment or the future. Any fear she harbored had been wiped away by her desire for him.

Maybe it was the hovering presence of death that urged her to rise up and drink every drop of life while she could. Or perhaps the ever-present sexual tension between her and Trey had finally broken, leaving no other choice but to fill herself with him. His scent, his strength, and every other thing she'd been dreaming of.

The velvet slide of his lips on hers was all that mattered now, and she didn't care what motivation had brought her here. It was exactly the place she wanted to be.

The fire between them burst into a roar to rival the one blazing in the hearth. Eve didn't know if the heat on her skin was from those flames or Trey's hands. Everywhere he touched seemed to burn and throb, pushing her to take more. She was greedy for him now, and couldn't stop if she tried.

She lost herself in the sensations surrounding her. Shadows danced with light, warmth raced over her skin, and the quilt was so soft as Trey lowered her to it. Lust was in full control as they stripped, desperate to slake the hunger for each other.

Eve tasted and ravished, exhilarating in the feel of his hard, muscular shoulders before stroking down the length of his back. She wanted to test every inch of him but kept losing her focus when his hands or mouth found and teased one of her secret places.

She arched up and moaned as her body found itself on the path to fulfillment with a pleasing ebb and flow of tension she knew would lead to release. "Trey," she said his name on a gasp as he continued to drive her closer. Rubbing, tasting.

He raised up and nudged her thighs apart with his own, "Oh, no you don't," he warned her. He pressed the thickness of himself against her but held back long enough to say, "The first time we're going there together."

His mouth found hers as he braced himself and slid inside, stretching and filling her with exquisite pressure. Together they rode, wildly pulling and straining, their bodies slick and fused into one. The brightness of the sun burst inside Eve as they rose and fell inside that magical place with love and pleasure crashing over them again and again.

When Eve found her way to Trey's neck, she hid her face against his warm skin. She could only manage short, hot breaths as she relaxed against him, still clinging to his body and what they'd made together.

Trey held her close until dawn broke and the embers in the

fireplace began to fade. Any time she stirred or woke in fear, she found herself locked tight in his embrace. Nothing could hurt her. Here at last was a refuge, a peaceful retreat.

A bird cried to announce the sunrise, but Eve nodded back off, reassured by Trey's presence and finally nightmare-free.

~~~

The killer's fist burst through the plaster of his wall, causing an immediate rush of anger and regret. He had to control himself and the rage. He was too close to lose control.

He had been even closer at her party, near enough to trace a hand down her lovely skin. The golden skin that would well up with precious drops of blood. He had been waiting years for a chance to rip and shred her soul. It should have been destroyed back then, on that long ago Halloween. As his had been.

He'd gone to her house again tonight, to watch and wait. Eve's dragon couldn't be at the door every second, and if he continued to be, well then something would have to be done about that as well.

All the windows had been curtained and shaded against him, but he could see the shimmer of fire behind two silhouettes. They were in there together.

Whore! He punched the fist into his other palm now. No reason to make more of a mess than he already had. He wouldn't let her affect his emotions ever again.

Soon. Soon she would know what she'd missed out on before, when she'd slipped away, taking advantage of the chaos and panic. She'd been rescued then, scooped away like an angel as he'd been forced to watch from the woods. And things had never been the same for him.

Halloween was only a few days away now, and debts would be paid. Recompense made to those who were owed.

But first he had another problem to take care of. The mouthy little reporter who had turned out to be such fun. She was tougher than she looked, and surprisingly entertaining, but she had served her purpose. It was time to move to the next phase of the plan.

The one that would take him another step closer to his prize. To his long cherished and awaited reward. His hallowed Eve.

Eighteen

Three large eggs, sugar, flour, and milk sat on the top of Eve's kitchen island. She put a finger to her lips and gathered the rest of what she needed, calling them by name as she plucked them from fridge or pantry. "Cocoa, vanilla, baking soda and powder, then the butter, softened of course." She smiled at herself and the silly game, basking in the glow of her favorite recreation.

She reconsidered. After last night, cooking was now her second favorite.

Her female heart fluttered at the memory of Trey's capable hands and the fulfillment of both body and soul that had overwhelmed her during their lovemaking. She was giddy, exhilarated, and falling fast into the spiral of love, so what better way to celebrate than by cooking a chocolate mousse torte?

Trey was upstairs showering, having fallen back to sleep after their early morning bout. Knowing full well he would have wanted her to wake him, Eve couldn't resist the opportunity to watch him as he slept, the sweep of black hair falling over his forehead and the usually stern features at ease while he slumbered. His full, firm lips reminded her how skillfully he had applied them as they'd lain entwined before the fire.

Eve shook herself, mentally and physically. Erotic chills surged through her before she cleared her head and returned to the task at hand. With the oven pre-heating, she prepared the jelly-roll pan with foil, then greased and floured it. After the mechanics were taken care of, she rubbed her hands together and set in to start the fun part.

She blended the butter and sugar together by hand, then streaked a finger through for a taste. Slipping her finger from her mouth, she again thought of Trey. The creation of food could also be sensual, if studied while in the proper frame of mind.

She had always respected the chemistry involved, Eve reflected while adding the eggs and vanilla, but had failed to see the complete indulgence of senses before today. Maybe Trey had introduced her to another level of awareness. Her skin and tongue certainly seemed to tingle in ways they never had before.

She continued to blend the ingredients, imagining how she and Trey had come together in a similar way. A little sugar, a little spice, and apply some heat. They had most definitely created something new in the lost hours of the night.

"If this is what true love feels like, it's no wonder romantic poets always sound so fanciful," she told the bowl before setting it in place beneath the mixer. The cherry red blender had a place of prominence in the kitchen. It was a bold splash of brightness in her earth-toned kitchen, but it had been Nan's. Plus, Eve had dipped her toe into Hades to get it from the basement, so she kept it out on the counter as a sort of talisman. An obscene gesture to the evil spirits of the world.

"Take that, boogeyman," she said, punching the button to start the whir and spin.

"Dare I ask?" Trey said from the doorway, startling Eve so that she slapped her hand to her chest. He was wearing black jeans with bare feet and bare chest, and toweling his hair, still wet from the shower. He looked good enough to eat.

"Just telling off the bad guys," she said with a shrug.

"Is that a part of the ritual?" He moved closer, watching as she slowly added milk and flour to the bowl, alternating between the two. "What are you making?"

"Do you like cake and chocolate?"

"Never turned either down." He kissed her cheek and draped the towel over one shoulder. "Looks good."

"It will be," Eve stated, not with ego, but with the surety that came from years of practice and reward. "I was in the mood."

Sitting on one of the stools, Trey said, "I hope this doesn't offend you, but how about we order a pizza?" He held his breath as if he expected her to respond with the temper of a television chef and hurl something at his head.

"Yum. You said the magic word."

He heaved a sigh of relief that made her laugh.

While Trey looked up the number for delivery, Eve spread the batter in the pan and started the mousse. Trey read the morning paper while she worked, and the two of them enjoyed a companionable silence. No mention of nightmares or murder. The familiar mist of worry hung in the corners of the room as they went about daily life, but neither felt the need to point it out.

The doorbell shattered the calm, bringing their anxious eyes up to meet before Trey left to see who it was, pulling a shirt over his head as he walked. Lately, they never knew what to expect when visitors arrived at the door or the phone rang. Their world had become a constant waiting game, never sure when the next crisis would make its appearance.

He came back with a fidgety Thomas on his heels. It looked like the crisis had arrived.

Eve could tell when trouble was brewing, and the younger man had a witch's kettle behind his green eyes. He shifted from one foot to the next and cast worried glances at Trey. "Eve, can I talk to you a minute? It's important."

"Of course." She caught Trey's eye herself, and he nodded to show he understood.

"I'll be getting dressed," he said, leaving Thomas and Eve alone.

"Sit," she ordered, pointing to the stool, "and tell me what's wrong."

"Please don't get mad," he pleaded.

Now Eve was growing concerned. "I can't promise that, but I will listen to what you have to say. Have you done something wrong? Something you think will make me angry?"

"No. No. It's just...I know you don't know me that well, and I want to keep my job." He began twisting the edge of his blue sweatshirt in his hands.

Eve walked over and put a hand on his shoulder. "Then tell me. It can't be that bad."

After a great gulp of air, he said in a rush, "The police brought me in for questioning last night. About those murders."

Eve's head reeled. This was not what she'd expected him to say. Now that she knew the current murders were related to those of her childhood, anyone the detectives considered a suspect was someone Eve should stay far away from.

She briefly considered calling for Trey, but let the snakes in her stomach settle down and took a long hard look at Thomas before changing her mind. He was miserable and terrified, and there was no reason to doubt his sincerity. Still, it was a relief to hear Trey's footsteps on the stairs.

"Why would they do that?" she asked, getting Thomas a soda to help put him at ease. She needed to hear everything.

"I told you how my brother knew the guy that got killed, remember?"

Eve nodded and went back to the mousse. It helped to have her hands busy and her focus on anything other than her young employee, who just might be more than she'd bargained for.

"Turns out I have a class with that girl who was taken from the college, and I didn't even know. I swear," he added when she lifted a doubtful brow. "I didn't even recognize her picture in the paper. I guess I just didn't pay attention in class. I mean, it's a seven-thirty class that I cut half the time, and sleep through when I don't."

That, Eve thought, sounded perfectly plausible. "It doesn't

seem like much. Not enough for the police to actually take you down to the station."

Trey walked through the door in time to hear the tail end of what she'd said, and his sudden stillness told her he was on point at the mere mention of police questioning. "Care to fill me in?" he asked.

If Thomas had looked nervous before, he now bordered on petrified. She was afraid he would rip his shirt any second.

"And I work for Eve," he told Trey in a panic, as if that would explain everything.

"I see. That might be a justifiable nail in your coffin, put together with the others," Eve said, holding a placating hand up to Trey. "It's fine. I'm fine." Then to Thomas, "You're not fired, and I'm sure you won't be. Just go home, and don't worry about it. I doubt I'll be working much until the killer is caught, but if I do, I'll let you know."

"I promise. It's not me." Thomas pleaded his case one last time, but was heading out the door.

"Thomas," Eve said, making him pause in his retreat. "Regardless, you need to be careful. Keep your eyes open, and don't go anywhere alone."

"You think this guy would come after me?" He flipped the hood of his sweatshirt over his head in preparation for the cold. "Why would he?"

"I don't know." She couldn't explain why the killer was targeting anyone, but there had been one other boy kidnapped from the carnival and imprisoned with Eve and the others. The ones who had died. If the murderer was recreating the past, the next victim could be another male. "Just be cautious. For me."

Since she smiled with the last, Thomas grinned back with the hope that he was still in good standing. "Sure. No prob."

Trey kept an eye on him until he was gone, then turned to interrogate Eve. Gone was the tender, passionate man who'd worked her into a frenzy between her cotton sheets at dawn.

The soldier was back, fully suited up, and he wouldn't be put off.

"Now, I'll ask again," he threw out, stalking over to halt the hand that was still stirring chocolate and forcing Eve to meet his fierce eyes. "Care to fill me in?"

~~~

Crossing the leave-strewn grass between his house and Eve's, Trey readjusted the massive bag of puppy food on his shoulder while Max trotted beside, around, and between his black boots, hoping for a stray kibble. Though he'd originally bought the economy size for the purpose of saving money, he realized the little eating machine would probably empty it before month's end.

Max had quite an appetite, but he was a growing boy. "Bet you're going to be big, huh? Judging by the size of those clumsy paws."

Excitement rolled across the puppy's back as he wiggled and jumped, encouraged by his master's voice. So much that he promptly tangled and tripped over said clumsy paws, then sat up to look around for whatever made him fall.

"Goofball," Trey said with an affectionate rub for the round golden head. The poor dog probably didn't even know where it lived, trailing back and forth between Trey's and Eve's. But since he seemed to be in a constant state of euphoria, Trey figured it didn't bother him much.

With a yip of pure delight, Max raced across the yard. Looking after him, Trey saw Eve at the end of her drive, reaching for the mailbox. She stopped at the sound of Max's barking, which escalated into a high-pitched squeal of ecstasy as he rolled into Eve's feet and lay belly-up waiting for her attention.

"For Pete's sake, Max, have some pride," Trey muttered to himself. But he had to smile as Eve crooned, and Max gazed up adoringly.

Maybe the pup had it right, and Trey should take note. Pride had gotten him into the mess he was in now. He'd omitted facts due to the insane notion he knew what he was doing and could handle it. He'd convinced himself Eve was better off not knowing.

In hindsight, the choice had been arrogant on his part and insulting to Eve. Now he'd slept with her and had crossed the line. Granted, it was a line he'd been planning to jump over since he'd first seen the woman that Nan's sweet little granddaughter had grown into, but he hadn't counted on doing so with a lie still between them.

The role he'd played had originally been a reasonable thing for a stranger to do. It had since twisted into a terrible deceit from the man she trusted. He should have told her the first time he'd touched her, but now he'd stalled too long and had to wait until the bastard who was stalking her was caught. He couldn't risk upsetting Eve and having her push him away while the killer was still out there. Then she would be alone and unprotected. That couldn't happen.

It still made him uneasy if he looked too hard at his reasons for guarding her so adamantly. Sure, it was the right thing to do, but he'd be forty kinds of fool to try and pretend there wasn't any more to it than duty. There was more. He just wasn't sure how much more.

I care for her. There. That hadn't been too hard to admit. In fact, it had felt pretty good. One of the many stones that always seemed to be sitting on his chest lifted.

But he wouldn't call it love. That was a weight of a different magnitude.

He looked again at the woman who'd given herself so freely to him, asking nothing in return except respect. She was tossing leaves up into the air so Max could attack them as they landed, then return to her for his hero's reward. He envied the puppy as it sat and let Eve rub its ears. Max had absolutely no trouble showing his feelings for Eve, and was basking in the return affection. *Yeah, maybe I should take lessons from the dog.*

Diverting from his intended route to the back, Trey swung in the other direction. He'd join in the fun of leaf-throwing and maybe steal a kiss or a nuzzle from the pretty lady himself.

His intentions were derailed. Again.

Eve looked up from the mail she had pulled out of the box, and Trey could see the weary sigh as it blew out of her defeated body. She held the orange envelope up with terror in her eyes but steel in her spine. "We got another one."

Anger surfaced then, and Eve dropped the other mail on the ground to free both hands. She tore into the envelope, her face clouded with rage. "Damn you. Damn you."

"Eve, wait," Trey called, setting the dog food down and coming to her side, but she already had the poem out and was reading. Her skin turned ashen, and she muttered, "So this is it."

"What is?" Trey grabbed it and looked it over.

Ladybug Ladybug
Fly away home
The world is on fire
And the children are gone

"He twisted the words again, putting his own message in them," he said quietly.

Eve bent to gather the scattered paper she'd dropped, moving like an automaton, bent on a function, a purpose, but with no life beneath. "It doesn't matter. It's done."

"What are you talking about? Do you know what this means?" He hurriedly read the lines again and returned his full attention to Eve. She was staring at him, her affect flat.

"Eve, tell me."

"He's not going to need a replacement for the Ladybug," she said.

Alarm gripped Trey in his gut. "Why not? Are you saying

he's done? He's finished?" The alternative didn't bear thinking, but Trey knew it was the only other answer.

"No. He has one more child to kill. The real one."

Eve was getting that faraway look, but she bit her bottom lip and sought out Trey with her eyes, visibly struggling to stay calm. "There was a little girl dressed as a Ladybug that night, and he still has to kill her."

Understanding flooded Trey and almost knocked him over. He thought he'd known fear before, but the man haunting Eve's steps was no longer skirting at the edges. No longer targeting faces in the crowd. "He's after the one that got away."

Eve nodded blankly. "That little girl was me."

Nineteen

The police were taking the threat seriously now, and probably thanking their blessed stars that Eve hadn't been hurt after their original dismissal of the poems and the trespasser at her home. Since she and Trey had turned over the last letter two days ago, they'd had a third wheel everywhere they went. Trey looked to his left as the unmarked car pulled up across the street.

The young cop hadn't liked it when Trey told him they were going to have lunch at Sturg's Diner, given the fact the man clearly disliked Eve, but Trey wanted to scope Sturg out for himself.

Since Eve and Trey were glued together like epoxy, she wasn't thrilled either. "I don't really want to deal with Sturg just now." She reiterated her argument as they swung open the glass door and stepped inside. Aside from the customers' clothing, they had been transported to the days of boy crooners and ponytails.

Trey took in the décor and had a hard time picturing the man who'd come up with it as a murderer. "I need to get a feel for him, and I'm not leaving you alone. We're here, so let's get it done."

"Fine." Eve stalked to a booth and sat, her temper evident in each quick move. If he didn't know any better, Trey would say they were having their first fight as a couple. It sure had the markings of a lovers' spat. Hell, the woman had even parted with the classic line so often wielded by the softer sex. *Fine*, she'd all but hissed.

For some unexplainable reason, her reaction made Trey grin. In the midst of everything they were up against and the recon he was here to do, it still made him perversely happy. *You got problems, Rainwater. Serious problems.*

He dismissed the emotional response and joined Eve. Sitting across from her in the cherry-red booth, he looked around for the cook, eager to judge Sturg's reaction first hand.

When he didn't see him, Trey returned his scrutiny to Eve and her beautiful face, even though her forehead still crinkled with pique. It wasn't the first time he'd experienced her foul mood. Since the last poem, she'd ping-ponged between being unruffled and completely tranquil to throwing flames from her eyes.

And she hadn't cooked a thing. That worried him most of all.

Constantly looking over their shoulders was keeping them both on edge, but despite the frayed nerves, they came together at night to escape and to discover. Their lovemaking was often a gentle search for comfort and security, a tempered storm. Other times it was a battle as much as a truce. A fury of devouring and pulling, each overcome by the desire they could never seem to satisfy.

The more Trey tasted of Eve, the more he wanted. She had become an addiction, and he was quickly coming to realize he would do whatever necessary to get his fix. He couldn't entertain the thought of giving her up.

Not only the sex, but something else. That thing he still didn't want to inspect too closely. The smile that brought an extra warmth to the blue of her eyes, the one he told himself she saved just for him. The pull to touch her when she was near, just a hand on hers while they sat watching T.V. And that he didn't mind her leg thrown over him at night after a lifetime of being a you-keep-to your-side-and-I'll-keep-to-mine sleeper.

He was scouting new territory now for sure, and the enemy

was as foreign to him as the emotions he was experiencing. He still saw any entanglement with a woman as something to be avoided, even if it did come in a package with silky hair of gold and lips that would tempt the gods.

Trey studied Eve's delicate hands as her fingers drummed on the table. Too much going on inside her for him to add any more. He just needed all of the drama to be over, then he could figure it out. And he could come clean with Eve.

When she'd gotten the last note, she'd wondered over Thomas's visit. "Surely he has nothing to do with it," she'd said. "Why would he be so obvious as to leave the letter in my mailbox on the very day he came to assure me he wasn't involved?"

She'd finally shaken off the idea, convinced it was all coincidence, but not until after a tirade about how the whole business was making her paranoid, and until the killer was caught, there was no one she could really trust. There was every reason to believe it was the man from her past, but who knew for sure? What if he was working with someone?

After she'd blown out all her steam, Eve had burrowed into Trey's chest, shaking and holding onto him as if he were a sturdy oak standing firm in the tornado that was her life. "I'm so glad I have you. That I can trust you," she'd whispered.

And the words had been a knife to his heart.

He didn't want the truth to hurt her at the end. And now, he didn't believe he could stand to lose her. What had he gotten himself into? Hopefully, she would understand, and forgive him for the omission. He preferred to think of it as a pesky detail left out due to its insignificance and not the lie that had wormed its way into betrayal.

"There he is," Eve said, jarring Trey so he tensed and looked around the diner.

"Where?"

"Where he's supposed to be. In the kitchen." She had yet to get over her mad if the sarcasm was any indication. She continued to stare through the large opening into the back where the burly man they'd come to test worked swiftly to add the final touch to an order before setting it on the counter.

When he glanced up to call the waitress, his eyes fell on Eve. His lip lifted in a snarl.

"I think you're right. He doesn't like you," Trey said, though he didn't consider the man a threat. Sturg's demeanor was that of a wayward teenage boy who spouted obscenities rather than handle controversy with logic. Trey knew the type and lifted his hand in a wave before smiling and gesturing for the man to come out.

"What are you doing?" Eve hissed through her teeth.

"You'll see."

When Sturg came to stand beside them, hands wiping on his apron as if in preparation for a fight, Trey armed himself with nothing more than a smile. "Sturg, good to meet you. Trey Rainwater," he said and stuck his hand out to shake.

Tentatively, Sturg took it, eyes shifting to Eve as if expecting a trick.

Trey gave him a firm grip to convey force, but let go just in time to turn the man's attention to friendly words. A mixed signal would help cloud what he suspected was an already foggy mind. "I brought Eve here so she could apologize in person."

Trey had heard of people being agog before, but Eve's expression was worthy of a whole new word. Before she could speak, he added, "She forgot to invite you personally to her Halloween party and was too embarrassed to mention it. I told her she should just come in and swallow her pride. A professional courtesy, you might say, since you are in the same business."

Eve's mouth was shut now, but she still looked ready to choke him. Trey kicked her under the table and lifted a brow to encourage her to play along. He could see her teeth gritting before she pulled out a timid smile for Sturg.

"It was an oversight on my part, and I hope you weren't

offended," she said. Trey tapped her foot with his until she added, "It was very rude of me."

As if on cue, the man responded as Trey had predicted. Smugness oozed from every pore, and he literally tucked his thumbs behind the straps of his apron before tilting back on his heels. "I thought so, but I am surprised to hear you admit it.

Though she was probably choking on the words, Eve evidently saw the wisdom in allowing Sturg to feel superior to her and laid it on a little more. "I hope you can forgive me. Maybe we can start fresh." Her blue eyes pleaded, and Trey thought she deserved an award.

"Well." Sturg took his time responding. "We'll have to see." He inclined his head to Trey as if they shared some secret then returned to his kitchen, a swagger in his stride, and sent their waitress over as he went.

Eve glared at Trey but firmed her mouth as if unsure whether or not to be mad. "I hate to say it, but that might have worked. Whatever possessed you to make me grovel, though?"

Trey lifted a shoulder carelessly. "I know the type."

"You don't think he's a threat? Not involved with the murders?"

Trey waited until the woman in her pink frilly uniform set their drinks on the table and took their orders before answering. "Let's just say I feel better having met him, but that doesn't mean I'm letting my guard down." He sipped his tea, grimaced, and reached for the sweetener. "I like knowing what to expect and where to expect it from."

"And from Sturg?" she asked.

"You'll probably see a new side of him."

Eve pressed her lips together. "I hope so, but don't expect me to keep that act up all the time. He should enjoy the moment while it lasts."

Trey rubbed her foot one last time, in affection as much as to tease. She shook her head as her mouth curved despite itself and grumbled, "Whatever."

They ordered to suit their tastes, she a salad and he a burger, but decided to share a dessert. They were still licking the apple pie from their lips when Eve's phone rang. Their small slice of calm came to an abrupt end when Eve looked at the screen. "It's Detective Curtis."

She answered and spoke in clipped short bursts. "Why me? Can't you tell me more?" She snapped the device closed after a few more noises of agreement and one, "Thank God," then looked at Trey with a mix of confusion and distress on her face. "He said it was no one in my family or a friend," she said.

"Back up. What did he want?"

Her eyes welled up, and she gripped his hand. "He wants me to come to the morgue. To identify a body."

~~~

Eve couldn't stop shaking, and the vibrations scattering through her bones were due to more than the chilly basement level where bodies were stored.

Cement walls, painted a redundant gray, absorbed the thin lighting from overhead bulbs, creating a sickly combination that only added to the repugnance of the place. There was no call for bright, cheery colors here, as the residents were long past the ability to appreciate their environment.

She should have been encouraged by the cause for her visit, but the grisly death of Mandy Pickerson overshadowed any sense of hope. Hope that he too was dead.

Two bodies had been found near a burning shack on the county outskirts. The kidnapper's attempt to cover evidence eventually led to his discovery, though his punishment had already been dealt. Mandy had seen to that.

It would take time to outline the sequence of events and how the dual deaths had transpired, but one thing was clear. At some point, Mandy had landed a blow to her captive's head, causing a "subdural hematoma," according to the medical examiner.

Reston had been more blunt. "He probably didn't even know he was dying as he hauled Mandy's body out to his car. It's called the talk and die syndrome, by some. One minute you're fine, then poof, you're dead." Reston had looked mildly amused when reporting the news to Eve and Trey, the first real hint of emotion they'd seen from the slick detective.

And that was how they'd been found. Mandy lying in the back of the vehicle with her legs dangling out, and her killer on the ground below, never having finished the deed. Some might call it poetic justice, but Eve just wanted confirmation it was the same man. The one who'd taken her and stuffed her in a cage, forcing her to see the cruelties he'd performed on the other children.

In part, she'd been lucky he'd never gotten around to her. Other times, she envied the ones who had died. They hadn't had to live with his face haunting them their entire lives, or with the memories of butchery that were as crystalline as reality. The visions, she prayed, would die along with him. If it was the right man.

There would be a comparison of his DNA to that found at the crime scene years ago, but Curtis and Reston agreed Eve should identify him if she could. Forensics would take days, and they wanted everyone's minds at ease, especially Eve's.

She could tell Detective Curtis still needed to rescue the little girl brought up from the dungeon of horrors so long ago. And Eve would gladly let him. Though she quaked in her brown boots as she walked with Trey, optimism somehow bloomed in the cold and surreal world of the morgue. She clutched Trey's jacket as they came to a stop outside a metal door.

"You ready for this? He'll have aged, but there's no damage to his face. You should be able to recognize him." Detective Curtis put his hand on the long door handle and paused for her confirmation.

Eve met his eyes. "I've seen his face countless times in my head. I remember what he looks like." She waited until he pushed down on the knob and let the steel swing open then took a deep breath and let go of Trey's arm. She marched forward to face her own personal demon.

The white sheet bulged in various places, as one might expect it to, but her focus was on the top, where she pulled off the sheet to reveal his head. The wicked face from her visions was relaxed, seemingly at peace, and Eve found the notion acutely distressing. "Wherever your soul is right now, I hope it's being torn apart and burned, over and over again. Like you did to them."

Her voice shook with emotion and she had to turn away, rushing to the nearest sink. The rage that burst out of her depths had been forceful enough to bring nausea along with it. It wasn't fear, sadness, or even the smell of a newly deceased body that caused her illness.

Years and years of jumping at shadows, avoiding dark underground rooms, and hiding her eyes from the images of mutilated children, these were the things that seemed to be clawing their way out of her chest. Evil was purging itself from her body and felt like it wanted to take her guts along with it.

Trey's arms were around her, his hand pulling back her hair. "Get it out. I'm here. I've got you."

Eve let him take the bulk of her weight, as she barely had the strength to cling to the edge of the long counter. She thanked heaven the sink was empty and clean. The roiling nausea might have been thrust into action if any leftovers from previous autopsies had been visible.

After a moment, her breathing eased and her stomach felt lighter. She found the strength to stand by herself, but didn't mind the continued presence of Trey's firm grip. She faced the detectives and nodded, though she was sure they needed no clarification. Her reaction had been answer enough.

In consideration, they had already re-covered the body, and

Trey herded her out the door when Curtis jerked his hand. No one wanted her to go through any more than she already had. Without speaking, Eve and Trey walked at a clip to the stairs, never slowing until they cleared the first floor and were in the lobby, surrounded by soothing coral and blue tones, chatting people, and confirmation of life. It did go on, and now, Eve realized, so would hers.

A new sensation spread from her core and out through her limbs. She couldn't pin it down with only one name, there were so many. Joy, freedom, justice. Her mouth spread into a grin before she could help it. "I should feel morbid, being this happy after what I just did." She put a hand to her mouth and looked at Trey. "But I don't," she whispered, grinning even wider.

Trey raised a brow, a cross between concern and relief. "Let me see if they need anything more, then we'll go."

She nodded. "Good. Because I'm hungry. No," she added and laughed, crossing arms to hug herself. "I'm starving."

TWENTY

It had been a treat to have someone serve her for a change, Eve thought as she and Trey made themselves comfortable in the kitchen. They'd just returned from eating out, and the Italian setting, complete with cracked walls, vineyard murals, and candles dripping onto green bottles had been the backdrop for a dinner that could only be described as celebratory.

Even Trey had passed on his usual beer to share an expensive bottle of wine with Eve. They'd stayed late and laughed long, each keeping to casual topics for the occasion, neither rushing back into serious conversation or hovering over nasty details best forgotten.

People had suffered and been murdered, but the fiend was now dead. Their corner of the world was a better place for it. There was no need to dwell on the past, but Eve knew there was unfinished business between her and Trey. To move forward, she had to put the memories to bed for good.

"Coffee?" she asked him as she started to measure the grounds. The sky outside was cloudless and still. The moon had a bare sliver of darkness on its left side, waxing toward the full moon that would be just in time for Halloween.

And that thought no longer paraded little cold men through her nervous system as it would have a mere three weeks ago.

"A little late for that, don't you think?" Trey said, settling himself on a stool. The kitchen had become their favorite meeting spot, war-planning room, and overall getaway from the world.

She held up the container. "Decaf."

"In that case." Trey motioned for her to fill it up.

Since he was coming to know her almost as well as she did herself, Eve guessed his acceptance was an open door for her to tell him whatever was on her mind. She took down her favorite red mug and handed him the usual black while setting out creamer and other niceties for the ritual. "I want to tell you what happened," she said, casting off the frivolous mood they had enjoyed all evening.

Trey nodded. "I hoped you would. When you were ready," he added, inclining his head.

"I don't know how quickly I would have made it to this point, but today was...well, cathartic is the best I can do, though it only scratches the surface. Years of therapy and self-psycho-maintenance couldn't do what seeing his dead, white face did for me." Eve shut her eyes. "That sounded pretty heartless."

"It sounded honest," Trey told her, "and I hope you know you can tell me how you feel. Don't censor it or worry what I'll think. You're being more delicate than I would anyway."

"Oh... well." Breath rushed out of her in relief. "Okay, I won't say I'm sorry for being glad he's dead. He brought nothing to the lives of others but misery. He was a thief, of children and their innocence, and he destroyed so many families who were left to imagine what went on in his hellholes. To wonder what their loved ones suffered before..."

Trey reached for her hand now but said nothing. Offering a weak smile of gratitude, Eve put her other hand over his, then pulled free to fill their cups. She needed something to hold on to when she told Trey about the worst days of her life. Something other than him, because she wanted to stand strong as she did so, and his comforting arms just might encourage her to hide away again.

He would give her that, she knew, but she also understood it wasn't what she needed. There was still a sickness clinging to her insides, one last tumor to be cut away, and only her hand could do the cutting.

"We were in the woods. The trails there had been converted into a haunted forest for the festival. Ghosts, witches, nothing too scary or violent as we were all still in elementary school. Since parents and faculty were dressed in costumes and scattered around the grounds, no one kept a constant eye on us." She stirred her coffee languidly, seeing the faces of her friends instead of the swirling caramel color of the drink in front of her.

"He was wearing a mask and outfit similar to one of the teachers. He came at us from out of the woods and told us to follow him, that there was more to see on the other side. He gave us candy." Eve frowned now. "If we'd only said no, but what kid turns down a treat? He was counting on that."

"The candy was drugged," Trey said, keeping a steady eye on Eve as she continued.

"It was. I remember feeling dizzy and sitting down in the leaves. The forest floor was covered, and I remember thinking how cold and crunchy it was. I was afraid to fall asleep because of bugs." She made a harsh sound, laughter choked with regret. "I would have gladly stayed with the worms and beetles if I'd known."

When Eve faded into silence, Trey watched with concern, then urged her to go on. "I know it's hard, but you're halfway there." He didn't touch her or offer words of sympathy, as either would have caused her to cave. Instead he waited.

She could feel the solidarity between them. Trey despised her tortuous walk down memory lane as surely as she did, but he put those feelings aside to be her constancy, her security. Eve would channel his strength and forge ahead. Like he said, she was halfway there.

Shaking off the bitter chill as if she were still lying in that cold forest, Eve sipped her coffee before continuing. "I woke up in a cage. That was what I noticed first. There was some sort of wire mesh stretched between wooden planks. The cells, I guess that's what you'd call them, were just large enough for us to lie on our sides in a fetal position or to crouch down, but we couldn't stand or stretch out fully. I don't know if he was cheap, lazy, or if it was all part of the torture."

Eve lifted her eyes to Trey's. "Because that's what it was really all about. He liked to make us uncomfortable first then add new levels slowly. Our fear gave him the biggest rush, I think, because he chose one child first to start with and didn't move on until..."

When she stopped, Trey gave her a moment then said, "Until they were dead."

Eve winced. "I was going to say when he was finished, but it amounts to the same thing. We all had to hear what was happening in the next room, and sometimes we had to watch. We knew when he was done because..." She coughed to force out the nausea that threatened again. "After he killed them, he brought their bodies back to their cells as if putting away dolls that had lost his interest."

Eve hardened herself as anger roared to life and burned away the last bit of terror. She would never forget what had happened in that basement, but she would never be slave to the memories again. "He never got to me. The last was one of the boys, and he was in the other room with him when the police came. I don't know what happened to either of them. The man escaped and they never found the boy's body. I'm sure his poor little bones are somewhere out there, tossed aside like garbage after that bastard had his pleasure."

She tilted her head. "I still don't know his name. I just think of him as the man or the killer." Rubbing her arms, she leaned against the island and studied the wood grain and the path it took under the shiny finish. "I'm not sure I do want to know."

"You don't have to." Trey stood and moved around to stand beside her. "You don't have to know or do anything else that relates to all of this. You've done enough."

"Not quite." She grabbed his hand and tugged him with her

as she moved toward the door that had once frozen her in her tracks. The gateway she had forced herself through, only to find a nightmare on the other side. "There's one more thing."

She dropped his hand and placed her own on the scratched glass knob. "This is my house, and I'm laying claim to it. All of it." Throwing open the door, she flipped the light switch with an air of arrogance and pounded down the wooden steps, telling any and all intruders she was there. Once she reached the bottom, Eve looked around, allowing her gaze to linger on one corner in particular. When nothing happened, she shut her eyes and willed the images to come forth, a foolhardy thing to do, but she was feeling reckless.

Still nothing but a chilly basement, shelving filled with storage items, and her grandmother's sea-green washer and dryer. Eve turned around triumphantly and looked up to see Trey standing at the top of the stairs with the light from her kitchen casting him in silhouette. There he waited for her to do what she had to do, but would have been down those steps in a heartbeat if she called.

Her hero. Her partner. The man she loved and who would love her back, even if he didn't know it yet.

With a very different type of swagger in her step, Eve climbed slowly. Once she reached the top, she placed a hand on Trey's chest to push him gently out of the way. She closed the door firmly behind her but left it unbolted.

Taking Trey gently by the hand, Eve led him down the hallway and up to the second story, toward her bedroom. With a gleam in her eye, she tossed a flirtatious smile over her shoulder as they walked. "Now. We still have some celebrating to do."

~~~

He'd been in this room before, had slept beneath the warm, down-filled comforter of blue and awakened to the sight of a feminine bedroom. Candles, flowers, and antique furniture said it belonged to a woman. A woman of classic tastes but an open mind, if you judged by the old carved bookshelves holding everything from *The Joy of Cooking* to a book on witchcraft Trey assumed had come from Gabrielle's store.

Though he was already accustomed to Eve's quirks as well as her bedroom, he was now in the midst of something entirely new. She moved lithely around the room, lighting the candles until the air grew heavy with a mix of sulfur and a sweet floral scent he couldn't name.

Eve was setting the scene for romance, but a tigress lurked behind her sky blue eyes. He'd never seen her like this but quickly decided he approved when she stopped to kick off her shoes and pull the thick band from her hair. She shook it out and lowered her head in a way that told him she would have what she sought from him tonight.

The thrill skittered down his abdomen and pooled in his loins. He would meet her head on.

He heard Eve call herself an Amazon at times, but the comparison was appropriate now. She was a wild woman who took no prisoners, and the thought of battling it out between the sheets found him hard and ready. They both needed an outlet, to ride along the jagged edge for the sheer abandon of it.

Her shirt was off in the space of a breath, her hands reaching for his buttons as her mouth slanted across his lips, greedy, searching, taking. The taste of her was hot and primal, her usual sweetness hidden beneath a slick feminine power that cried out for the taking. And take he would.

Trey fisted his hands in the silk of her hair, gripping the base of her head to hold her in place, so he could do some ravaging of his own. He stroked and teased with his tongue until she moaned and pulled away to attack the clothing that was still a barrier.

There were no loving strokes or contented sighs. Not this time. They grasped and pulled, using hands and mouths to find those places that would drive the other mad. When Eve was left in nothing but a small patch of pink cotton, an incredibly sexy excuse for underwear, he picked her up to lower her to the bed before inserting himself between her knees. He hovered above her, leaning onto his elbows to trail his open mouth across her stomach, nipping and sucking as he saw fit.

Eve gasped when two fingers skimmed beneath the band of her panties and followed the side of the cloth down, down, slowly enough to anticipate his destination yet heighten the sensitivity of the area as he circled and skimmed, never quite giving her what he knew she wanted. He lowered his mouth to the outside of the cotton and used his moist heat to push her further.

Eve's hips arched off the bed of their own accord. She was losing control, and he loved it. "Trey, please," she gasped, the quickness of her breath telling him she was almost there.

He pulled off the hindering fabric and used his tongue, his fingers to take her over the last crest until his name became a chant of gratitude and wonder. He could feel the strength of her climax and reveled in the moment when her thighs shook and her head fell back in rapture.

Eve's arms had barely hit the mattress in utter relaxation when Trey slid himself up to look into her eyes and settle himself between her legs. "Eve." He kissed her neck, her shoulder, bewitched by the woman who had become the center of his life. He waited until the haze cleared from her eyes and they met his with a communion felt only by lovers.

Somewhere inside him, a spring uncoiled, letting loose a flood of affection for her that rode along with the waves of desire and greed, the need to consume and own every part of her body and spirit.

Their gazes locked and held true as he drove into her, giving and taking fully. As she did. The rise and swell came again for her quickly, followed by a small but wicked smile. Trey was determined to see that look on her face one more time. When

Eve sobbed his name against his shoulder, he let himself go with her, shattering into a million pieces of light.

The two of them lay tangled in the soft white sheets, his darker skin tone flowing with the golden hue of Eve. They basked in the glow of the candles, content to be as they were.

Trey took one look at her face as she dozed, the sharp curve of her cheek and the shadow of lashes that rested there. With no warning at all, he felt his heart drop from inside to land there beside her. He swore her hand clutched lightly, briefly, as if knowing it was there for her taking.

Stunned, Trey looked about the room, but the dark offered no answer or solace. After weeks of fighting away Eve's worst fear, he now found himself confronting his own. *So much for being in control.* Somehow during it all, she had sneaked her way in, past all of his tried and true fortifications.

Somehow, she'd made him love her.

Twenty-One

"Here they come," Eve said, excitement shivering through her voice. She peered out the window of the living room to watch as a soldier, a fairy, and Spiderman turned to walk up her drive. They were her first official trick-or-treaters, and Eve was more than ready to hand out Halloween candy. For the first time in her life.

She'd debated over the many robotic and computerized options candy bowls came in these days, but settled on a large, plastic book of spells that cackled and spoke in a gravelly witch's voice when the lid opened. Trey had argued for the one with a hand reaching up through the treats, but Eve didn't want to scare any kids. She would hate to be responsible for making any toddlers cry.

Trey met Eve at the door but allowed her to do the honors. He was dressed in black, but that was all he'd committed to. He'd stated plainly that he'd dressed up once already for Halloween and had met his limit for the season. Eve, on the other hand, had opted for a brand new costume. She was riding high and basking in the thrill of ghosts and goblins, and wanted to make this a Halloween to remember. It was an attempt to reset and redefine this night for now and the years to come. She wouldn't forget her past, but it would never control her or cripple her again.

Throwing back her shoulders to display the scarlet cross of the Knights Templar on her white tunic, Eve put one hand on her plastic sword. She opened the door to the children and said,

"Halt! Who goes there?"

She was met with giggles and one exclamation of, "Cool!" The tiny soldier recognized one of his own. "Is that a real sword? Can I touch it?"

"You may," Eve said, still in her best man's voice, holding her faux weapon out for inspection. The little boy nodded gravely and pulled his toy gun out to return the favor. Eve declared it a "fine piece" and let the little girl in fairy wings open the candy box. The children weren't fazed by the creepy voice telling them to pick carefully. So much for being scary.

Once the kids had scampered back to their parents and Eve had closed the door, she threw herself into Trey's arms and hugged tight. "That was so fun!" She drew back to see him grinning with one side of his mouth.

"If that's what giving out candy does for you, then maybe we should order that horror movie after all." He leaned in and kissed her fully but briefly. "Maybe I'll get more than a hug."

"Maybe you will," she whispered. "If you are deemed worthy."

"I'll put my Sig up against your discount sword any day, old man."

Their next kiss was interrupted by a quick knock and Gabrielle swinging through the front door. "Oops. Sorry. Think you guys should go elsewhere? This part of Halloween is generally G-rated." She threw a thumb over her shoulder. "And your next group is coming up the walk."

"Out of my way," Eve said, brushing past Gabrielle to grab the candy. "I'm on."

Gabrielle lowered her head slightly and looked at Trey. "Is she serious?"

"More than." He studied Eve as she put her hands on her hips and gave the kids a show. He smiled at her antics. "But she's happy."

Gabrielle sighed and looked at her friend. "She is that."

"What's in the bag?" Trey asked, reaching for the paper sack.

"Provisions. What else?"

He glanced at Eve and back to Gabrielle's bag. "You didn't happen to bring any scary movies, did you?"

Eve turned just in time to hear the question and playfully punched Trey on the shoulder. "Be good, or I won't let you see what's under my chain mail."

Throwing her hands up, Gabrielle headed toward the kitchen. "That's way too much of a visual for me," she called back.

Trey watched her go then turned to Eve. "I just had a thought," he said.

"A clean one?"Eve asked dryly.

"Maybe we should set Gabrielle up with Sam."

Eve watched her friend sashay down the hall in tight black pants and leather boots. A leopard print top and cat ears on a headband completed the outfit. Eve lifted her eyebrows. "Gabrielle and shy Sam? Um, somehow I think she'd eat him up."

Trey took Eve by the hips. "I doubt he'd complain." He silenced her by moving in for another kiss.

Eve held on to his broad shoulders and breathed him in. The clean, woodsy smell was now familiar and always triggered pleasing memories. His scent had become her own personal aphrodisiac.

She had no idea how long they'd been locked together when the doorbell rang once again, but she was almost sorry to let go. Almost. She was actually enjoying all the spooky stuff and the wild costumes people came up with. She and her best friend and the man she was crazy about were dressed up and reveling in the spirit. Life was good.

Trey pulled back with a wink and jerked his head toward the door. "Go get 'em, Sir Eve."

~~~

By nine o'clock they'd been cleaned out, and even the mint

chewing gum Gabrielle had scoffed at was gone. The streets were clear of trick-or-treaters for the most part, so Eve finally turned the porch light off. She left the decorations lit to enjoy the mood a little longer. "I can't believe I've missed out on this every year. The kids were so cute, especially the tiny ones."

"I know," Gabrielle said. "Those three little pigs were precious."

"And their dad as the wolf. What a great idea." Eve pulled off her tunic and the belt holding her sword. "I'm ready to come out of this stuff, though. It's getting hot." She was left in a white long-sleeved T-shirt and matching stretch pants. "I'm ready for the next stage."

"The next stage?" Trey asked.

"Fear fest on the big new T.V." Eve had splurged on one more purchase, a flat screen for the den.

"Yes!" Gabrielle was a fan of any movie starring werewolves, phantoms, or slashers. "I'll go start the popcorn." She took three steps then skidded to a halt. "Oh, no. I think I left it at home."

"You sure?" Eve asked, moving with her toward the kitchen.

Gabrielle checked her bag but came away with a frustrated sigh. "Yep. I suddenly realized I left the box in my cabinet. We can't have a monster marathon without popcorn." She removed the cat-eared headband and tossed her brown curls over her shoulder. "I'll run get some. I can probably find a gas station that's still open."

"No." Eve turned steadfast eyes to Trey and asked him, "Would you mind? I think it's time we peeled away from each other for a few minutes. I have to start being alone anyway. Might as well jump in the deep end." She looked at Gabrielle then back to Trey. "Besides, Gab will be here, and it won't take you more than twenty minutes."

Trey wanted to refuse. He hated the idea of leaving Eve by herself, especially on this night, but what could he say? He didn't want to make her feel unsafe. She'd had too much of that. The murderer was dead and could pose no more threat, so Trey just had to get used to the idea of having Eve out of his sight. They would both have to return to normal eventually, but daylight hours on a regular Tuesday afternoon would have suited him better.

He might as well get it over with and the quicker the better, even if only for his peace of mind. "What flavor, butter or caramel?" he asked the women, lifting his jacket from the back of a chair on his way out.

Eve and Gabrielle answered simultaneously. "Both!"

Trey smiled and mumbled to himself, "Of course. What was I thinking?" He exited into the bracing October wind and scanned the neighborhood for anything off kilter. His instincts were humming, but he couldn't say why.

He would make sure he was back in fifteen minutes or less, and Eve would never have to know he drove ninety down Main Street to do it. He was well aware of the damage a man could do in seconds, much less minutes, and it didn't bear thinking of. He was probably being paranoid and overprotective, but something about the pewter clouds gliding over the face of the moon set his hairs on end.

The wind chose that moment to whip into a frenzy and an owl hooted in response. Trey decided not to waste any more time but jumped in his car and backed onto the road.

Maybe he could make it in ten.

~~~

"He's got it bad for you, you know?" Gabrielle sat next to Eve on the couch and fanned out the DVDs on the coffee table. "Any man who doesn't question a female ritual, and on top of that, actually contributes to it...that's a man worth keeping."

"He's full of surprises," Eve admitted. "His tough exterior finally started cracking, after considerable effort on my part. Just enough for me to get a peek of what's inside. We're still taking our time, because, well…look what we've been going through. We need to let things settle and see where we end up."

"Bullshoot." Gabrielle said before taking a sip of her diet soda. "You heard me," she added when Eve croaked a laugh. "Trey didn't have to stick around for the festivities. Most men would have quietly eased their way out when things started getting intense. Plus, I see the way he looks at you."

Eve considered her friend's words and felt a silly smile spread across her lips. She was beginning to imagine a life with him, in Pine Creek. She'd really done a one-eighty since she'd first come home. At first, she could barely wait to leave again. Now, she actually wanted to stay and be a part of the community. She got all warm and fuzzy inside when she thought of Trey moving into her house, waking up with her each morning, and making love to her each night.

Now that she wasn't worrying about a stalker or serial killer, she could enjoy the start of something real between her and Trey. Maybe bask a little in the feelings she had for him. Her insides got all warm and achy whenever she pictured his crooked smile or the way his eyes went molten just before he…

"Please wipe that goofy look off your face. I still have eating to do." Gabrielle nudged Eve.

Eve grinned. "Jealous?"

"Hmph."

Eve raised one curious brow. "So, have you had any special vibes lately?" She remembered what Gabrielle had told her the day they'd gone shopping. She hoped the dire premonition had been about the stalker and that it had died along with him.

Gabrielle took a long drink, coughing a little after she swallowed. "Oh. I forgot all about that. Guess you're all clear."

Eve was no soothsayer, but she recognized telltale eye avoidance when she saw it. She wanted to press her friend on the matter, because Gabrielle was suddenly nervous. Eve didn't think Trey would appreciate psychic mojo or feminine intuition, so she'd specifically waited until he left to bring up

Gabrielle's prediction. Now she was glad he wasn't here, since she might have to do some arm-twisting. Her friend was back-pedaling. Hard.

Barking erupted from the back porch, breaking into Eve's train of thought. She stood in a rush. "I forgot Max. He's still outside." She shrugged one shoulder. "We were afraid he'd jump on the kids. Or wet on them."

Eve marched down the hallway, yelling over her shoulder. "Don't think you're off the hook, either." She intended to find out whatever Gabrielle was trying so hard not to say.

Max was aquiver when she opened the door to let him in. He nuzzled and licked her hands, filled with the simple delight of having someone's attention. "It's getting cold out here, isn't it? Maybe you should come in by the fire and protect us from the boogeyman or Martians, or whatever we decide to watch."

A crunching noise made Eve jerk to attention, and Max stilled in her hands, his ears cocked to listen. He'd heard it, too. The puppy gave a whimper that turned into a growl before shooting off high-pitched barks toward the back yard.

Now Eve was the one standing still, trying to focus on any stray noise. An ice cold bug seemed to skitter across her scalp as she stared into the dark. The blue lights were on in the pretend graveyard but didn't cast their glow very far. She couldn't see anything. Nothing moved.

After a few seconds, she shook herself and picked the puppy up to take him inside. "Guess it will take a while. I've been jumping at noises so long it's become habit." The dog shivered, staring dolefully over her shoulder. He yipped one more time.

Eve turned to close the door behind her, but it burst open and slammed into her side, the momentum pushing her forward and off balance. She felt her shoulder get hit hard, saw the dog leap from her arms, but she was still falling and could only scramble to right herself.

She didn't look behind her to see whoever had forced his way inside her home. Her brain had hazed over with an alarming shade of orange, thrusting her into flight mode. Somehow the nightmare was here again and breathing the stench of death all over her.

A hand clutched her arm to wrench her back, stopping her with a jerk that rattled her teeth. He was trying to pull her out the door. She felt a scream punch from her diaphragm when his other hand grabbed her hard around the waist.

Thrusting her arm out to grab onto the counter, she knocked a vase of orange tulips to the floor, causing glass to shatter everywhere while water spread across her new hardwood floors. She struggled and strained as he dragged her with him, but in no time they were across the threshold of the back door. He smashed a smelly cloth over her mouth and nose.

"Eve? You okay?" Gabrielle rounded the corner at the far end of the hallway then stood with her mouth open and a shocked look on her face. "No!" she screamed, breaking out of her trance to race to Eve's aid.

The intruder thrust Eve to the side where she landed in broken glass and scattered flowers. Her vision was foggy at the edges from the drug she'd inhaled, but she saw Gabrielle lunge toward the man. He hit her with a fist in the chest then pulled something out from behind his back as she stood there stunned. As Gabrielle fought to catch her breath, he brought a black pistol down on her head once then sideways across her temple. The second blow sent her careening into the wall where she slid down into a heap. She was out cold and blood was already dripping from beneath her brown hair.

With renewed energy fueled by rage, Eve pushed herself up, ignoring the shard from the vase as it cut into her left palm. The man wore a clear plastic mask to distort his features, but Eve only saw a killer and the person who'd been torturing and harassing her for weeks. There was no doubt in her mind that the author of her poems stood before her now.

She glanced at Gabrielle and knew she had to make a choice. The bastard had a gun, and Eve wanted him and his weapon far away from her friend who lay unconscious and completely vulnerable. She brought her leg up and delivered a sound kick to his right kidney. She knew it would only buy her a few seconds. "You want me you spineless coward, so come on. You've been hiding the whole time, and you still are. Hiding behind a child's mask."

He whipped his head toward her, and through the small holes in the plastic Eve could see his eyes burning with hatred. He was sure to follow, but her time was up.

Without thinking, she sprinted out the back door and leaped down the steps. Her head ached mildly from the sickly sweet cloth he'd held over her face, but her eyes had cleared. Adrenaline and the cold night air helped sharpen her senses. She didn't have a plan other than to get out of the house, but he had a gun and would catch her any moment. She had to move fast.

Tearing through the headstones, she headed toward the woods, hoping the trees would give her some coverage. If she couldn't outrun him, maybe she could at least stay hidden until he gave up. Or Trey returned.

Trey. Oh, God. It wouldn't take long for him to make sense of the chaos left behind in Eve's kitchen, and with the back door open, he would know which way she'd headed. She needed his help but also feared for his life.

Eve was at the edge of the forest and still running fast when she felt and heard a presence at her back. Heavy footsteps were behind her, moving at a quicker pace, then she heard an expulsion of breath as the killer threw himself at her. He slammed into her back and tackled her, driving her already aching shoulder into the ground. They skidded across the lawn and Eve felt her face scrape across the dried grass and leaves.

Before she could attempt a struggle, the man flipped her over to straddle her mid-section, trapping her arms along her sides. His strong thighs clamped down while he grabbed her upper arms and rammed her head against the hard earth.

Eve's head swam from the impact, but she was able to watch as he slowly peeled away the mask. The action revealed a face she recognized.

"I've been waiting for this moment, Eve. Your turn is long overdue." He brought his mouth to her ear where he heaved ragged breaths and whispered, "Happy Halloween, bitch."

TWENTY-TWO

Eve filled her lungs to scream, but the killer pressed his palm over her mouth. Grinning with cruel enjoyment, he used his other hand to pinch her nose. She was already winded from trying to escape, so her lungs began to burn immediately, like two balloons full of heated metal. She was afraid he would kill her here in her grandmother's back yard, with a yellow October moon as the only witness.

When the suffocation became unbearable, he let go and laughed in a low rumble. "It's not going to be that easy. You and I are going to have some real fun before you set me free."

His words confused Eve, but she was too busy gasping the cool night air to worry about their meaning. His hands glided down her throat and over the curve of her waist before he bunched her shirt in his hands and pulled twice. "Get up. We have to get out of here before Trey comes back."

At the mention of Trey's name, Eve gathered her courage and stood, her legs still shaking from exhaustion and fright. "Who are you?" she croaked, forcing herself to stand taller, steadier. She wouldn't let him think she was intimidated. He would only take pleasure in her weakness.

He twisted her arm up behind her back and steered her toward the side of the house. Eve clenched her teeth instead of crying out then swallowed the bile that threatened. "I recognize you, but that's not what I mean. I'm not asking about your name. I want to know *who you are*."

He growled and jerked her arm higher, and this time a

whimper escaped Eve's mouth. She was afraid he would wrench her shoulder out of joint.

"Who am I?" He shook her, sending bolts of searing pain through her neck, arm, and upper body. "I'm the one who *didn't* get away."

Eve clenched her eyes tight in agony, but they flew open as comprehension dawned. "The cowboy," she said. You were the little boy dressed as a cowboy. But we didn't know. We all thought you'd been killed. That he hid your body."

"I wasn't lucky enough to die young like the others or get swept up by the police like you." He raised his voice now. "You should have been there, too! I could have done better with you, and he would have been satisfied!"

Eve's mind worked frantically, trying to put together the various pieces like a jigsaw puzzle immersed in water, the interlocking parts blurred and unfocused. "I don't understand. Why did you kill all those people? What do you want with me? I never knew you. I didn't do anything."

"You did everything!" He had worked himself into a rage, and his grip grew tighter, his breathing heavier.

Eve felt spittle fly from his lips to land on her cheek. "My arm," she said on a sob. She hated to beg, but everything in her shoulder felt like it was splintering into pieces.

"Sam!" The voice came from nearby, but Eve couldn't pinpoint the location. *Trey. You're here. You came back.*

The killer cursed under his breath then shouted, "Back off, Rainwater. I have the first claim on Eve. She belongs to me. She's always belonged to me."

Trey moved into a stream of moonlight, and Eve's chest tightened at the look on his face. Sam wasn't the only one here capable of brute force. Trey's stance was deceptively casual and his expression unreadable. His anger was disguised by calm, but vengeance lurked in the depthless black of his eyes. He was a walking weapon, controlled and deadly.

"How could you do it, Sam?" Trey asked his friend in a flat

tone. "And all right beneath my nose. I'll give it to you...I never suspected."

Sam let up on Eve's arm, and she blew out a relieved sigh. She still ached, but it was manageable. She kept her eyes on Trey moving in closer, his arms at his sides as he circled to keep Sam's attention on him.

"Sam," Eve said, licking her parched lips. "I don't understand. Tell me what happened. What do I have to do with it?" Maybe she could get him talking and keep him distracted. Trey would know when to attack, but Eve would do all she could to help.

"Yes, tell us about it, *Sam*," Trey said, his voice hard and low. "Or is that even your real name? Is this why you befriended me? Because I lived next to Eve's grandmother? How could you have known things would go the way they have, because I can't give you much credit for foresight."

Eve didn't know why Trey was mocking him, but she was afraid of the consequences. Trey either didn't know Sam had a gun, or he didn't care. "He's been planning this for a long time. Isn't that right?" she asked Sam, taking advantage of the fact he'd loosened his grip on her arm as he watched Trey.

"I didn't know if you would come in handy or not," Sam glared at Trey and gave a throaty laugh, "but it worked out particularly well. You fed me more inside details about Eve than you realized. I knew when and where she would be by checking in with you. And you were always unguarded with your good fishing buddy." He let go of Eve's arm to reach for his gun in a quick, fluid motion, pressing the barrel into her temple before she had a chance to react. "And where was your foresight, Rainwater? You let yourself get a little...distracted."

Eve could feel Sam tensing up again. He moaned near her ear, the sound barely audible and filled with both pain and wrath. "You have no idea what I went through," he said, rubbing his face against hers. "He was never satisfied, not without you. He was crazy before, but over time, our failures drove him completely insane. The torture never lasted long enough. The cries were never good enough. And then he would look at me."

"You killed him, didn't you?" Eve asked. "You set it up to look like he was responsible for the most recent murders, but it was all you. You killed him and Mandy, all of them." She tried to make her voice soft and sympathetic. They'd stopped moving toward the front of the house but were drenched in shadows. Her eyes weren't adjusting fast enough, and she hoped Trey was having more luck. She prayed that he had a plan.

"It was time for him to die, and the recovery of his body served a purpose." Sam took a deep sniff of Eve's hair then licked her jaw line. "When they found him, you thought you were safe. You left yourself wide open for me, just like I knew you would. You've been waiting for me, haven't you?" His voice was hoarse with some twisted type of desire, and Eve felt nausea twinge in her stomach.

"If you're going to shoot anyone, you'd better aim this way." Trey was trying to get Sam's attention. He was to their left, on the opposite side of the gun. "You'll only get off one shot, and it had better count." Leaves crunched as he stepped closer. "Or you're dead."

"You don't have anything to do with this, Trey. She owes me for what I went through. The training he put me through. Slicing people up takes practice if you're going to do it right." He tapped the gun against Eve's head then pressed it firmly under her chin. "But it never mattered how well I did or how many blonde girls we found. He was never happy, because none of them were her!"

Sam bit into Eve's neck, breaking the skin in several places, and she couldn't stop the cry that broke from her lips. He pulled away, but rammed the gun harder into the soft skin under her chin. "Do you know what he did to me then? Whenever it wasn't you?"

Trey was only a few feet away now, and whatever clouds had been blocking the moon were swept away, making them all visible in the eerie light. "Last chance, Sam. Let her go."

Eve knew something would break soon. Sam was becoming too unstable for Trey to risk waiting much longer.

Sam laughed again, only this time it sounded forced and sarcastic. "Oh, because you care so much?" he asked Trey. "Because you *love* our Eve?" He kissed Eve's neck where he'd bitten, making her wince. "Did he tell you he's been spying on you since you came to Pine Creek?" Sam asked Eve, motioning toward Trey with the gun.

Eve didn't know what he was talking about but risked a gentle shake of her head.

"He agreed to help that lawyer of your grandmother's. It was his job to make sure you didn't leave town. That you fulfilled your agreement to live here for a year." Sam's voice changed again, filled with hatred. "And he did a good job keeping you here, didn't he? He just kept you pinned down while he fucked your brains out."

As if the thought of it was too much, Sam started shaking and raised the gun to point it at Trey. "She's mine!" he yelled.

Eve was still shocked by what Sam told her but managed to throw her arm up and knock him off his aim, giving Trey the opportunity he needed to lunge forward. Sam had been holding Eve to him with his other arm, but he let go to meet Trey head on and regain control of his weapon. Eve had been straining against his hold, so she tumbled to the ground.

The gun went off, and she flinched before looking up to see the two men still locked in battle. Trey was skilled and a fury-filled package of strength, but Sam was fueled by his insanity and determination. He had nothing left to lose.

She wanted to help but was afraid she would only distract Trey. She sat there, watching as they fought. Trey maneuvered Sam into a weaker position with the gun pointed away from any of them, giving Eve hope the killer would finally be stopped for good. Trey seemed to be winning.

Sam roared suddenly and threw his head up to smash into

Trey's face. The momentary surprise cost Trey his grip on his opponent, and Sam slid out of his grasp just enough to angle his arm and point his weapon at Trey.

"No!" Eve screamed and tried to stand, knowing there was no way she could get there in time.

The men grunted and came together like two rams in a death match, and Eve heard Sam say, "She is *mine*," before the gun went off again. Silence followed the blast as the two men sagged against each other, heads bent forward.

Eve had no way of knowing who was hit, if anyone, but she rushed forward to do what she could. Trey's arm shot out to hold her at bay, and she could see his hand pulling away with the gun. He gave a small push, and Sam stumbled back a step before crumpling to his knees. His eyes were wide with the knowledge of impending death, but Eve could only stand there staring. A crimson Rorschach appeared on his chest, mesmerizing as it grew and spread.

Eve didn't rush to help and could summon no sympathy for her tormentor. An image flashed in her mind, a small boy dressed for Halloween, tears streaking his face as he waited in the cage across from Eve. She would always feel horrible about what had been done to that child, but she would forever hate the man he'd become.

Sam threw out his arm, clasping his hand as if trying to get to Eve. His final thought was still of her, and she knew then he would have never stopped. If she wanted to live, then she had to let him die.

The iron smell of his blood blew to her on a gust of wind, reminding her of another who lay bleeding. "Gabrielle," Eve cried. I have to call for help!" She bolted for the back and flew into the kitchen to help her friend. Gabrielle hadn't moved, and the utter stillness of her body terrified Eve.

She barely noticed Trey's absence as she dialed the phone on the wall, silently thanking her grandmother for keeping the land line. She spit out the details to the operator, giving her address first and stating they needed an ambulance and the police. As an afterthought, she requested Detectives Curtis and Reston be notified as well.

She left the phone hanging with the operator's voice telling her assistance was on the way. A downstairs linen closet held some towels, and Eve grabbed a couple of white ones then returned to press them to the bleeding. She didn't know anything about head wounds, and tears gathered in her eyes as she wondered what to do. Gabrielle had always been there for her, and now she might...

"He's dead." Trey had silently entered the room to make the announcement. He moved to kneel next to Eve. "You're doing good. Just keep pressure there."

He put a hand on Eve's shoulder, but his touch felt foreign. She had no idea who he really was. She shrugged him off, focusing her crying eyes on Gabrielle. "They're sending the police and an ambulance." She sniffed. "They should be here soon."

"I'll stay with you. I can give you a ride to the..."

"No." She cut him off. "I'll drive myself or call Lance." It sliced her heart to raise her eyes to his, but she could no longer afford to be in the dark. She had to know she was surrounded by people she could trust, and Trey had destroyed the faith she'd had in him.

How could he have become so ingrained in her life and never have told her the truth? Why hadn't she picked up on the hesitation or averted glances, both his and Kurt Dennis's? And her grandmother? Had she known what Trey would be doing? Had she asked him to watch over Eve...no, spy on her?

She'd taken him to her bed and shared herself like never before, and all the time she was nothing more than a job to him. Her mind roared, and her heart turned to stone as she considered the extent of his betrayal.

"When they get here, you can leave," she said, the words short and tight.

"Eve." He had the audacity to look wounded.

"Just go, Trey." When her mouth started to quiver, she firmed her jaw and said, "You did an excellent job, but your work here is finished."

Twenty-Three

Eve could still hear the beeping in her head. Though she'd only been allowed to visit Gabrielle for limited periods of time in the ICU, the mechanical tone of the heart monitor had been an incessant reminder of her friend's peril, and the phantom sound still punctuated her fear. Gabrielle had been moved to a med-surg bed, which was good, but until she woke as her normal self, Eve would worry.

She couldn't help but feel Gabrielle's injury was all her fault. If she hadn't insisted Trey leave for something as trivial as popcorn. If she'd responded the first time she'd heard movement in her back yard. If she'd done anything differently, maybe her lifelong friend wouldn't be lying in this bed with her face almost as pale as the hospital sheets.

Gabrielle had woken up twice but had talked in circles both times. Once she'd been violently ill and cried from the extra pressure the vomiting caused in her head. Eve had cried along with her before the nurse came and injected something into the IV line to ease Gabrielle's nausea. She had been diagnosed with a severe concussion, but luckily, no brain hemorrhage. Now they just had to wait and let her recover.

Which left Eve with plenty of time to think, to beat herself up, and to suffer the heartbreak Trey had left behind.

For the thousandth time she pictured his face on the day they'd met, his strong countenance and virile sex appeal. Or the way he'd tended to her so gently after finding her in a hysterical mess on the ground outside their homes. The way his hand traced the lines of her face and his dark eyes held hers as they made love.

She had known him then, for who he really was. She was sure of it. How could everything have been a lie?

Eve had called Kurt Dennis this morning, once Gabrielle had been downgraded and transferred. She'd asked him point blank if he had hired Trey to keep an eye on her. His answer had been a relief but even more of a puzzle. Trey had done it as a favor to Nan. Her grandmother had asked him to keep an eye on Eve, and he'd given his word. So how was Eve supposed to resent a man for being respectful to Nan and for keeping the promise he'd made to her?

As upset with him as she was...still...she also had to allow him a small amount of begrudging respect. And he'd never promised to risk his life. Gabrielle had been right about that. With a stalker and serial killer in the mix, not to mention Eve's little "attacks," most men would have left skid marks.

Trey had only dug his heels in.

A groan from the bed made Eve sit up and shake off her maze of confusion. Gabrielle was awake and looking at Eve, blinking her eyes as if clearing them. "Hey," she croaked. "Did we get him?"

Eve assumed she meant their attacker. "Yes." She leaned forward and clasped Gabrielle's hand. "Dead and buried. Well, soon to be buried. It was Sam all along, but we'll get into that later. You need to rest."

"Sam? The guy you wanted to fix me up with?" Gabrielle rolled her eyes. "Glad to see you think so much of me."

Eve smiled. "The guy Trey wanted to set you up with, but I vetoed it, just so you know."

Motioning toward the water bottle on her bedside table, Gabrielle sat up a little more in the bed. Eve pushed a button to raise the head up for support and helped her friend take a few sips.

Gabrielle looked around the room. "When can I get something

to eat?"

Eve's heart filled with warmth. "Feel like you can hold it down?"

"I feel like I could eat a buffalo. Now don't tease me. Where's my menu?"

After clarifying the doctor's order for a diet, Eve called in an order then went to get a bag of chips from a nearby vending machine to help tide her friend over. Eve was a beast if she didn't get to cook often enough, but Gabrielle became a monster of epic proportions if she didn't get fed regularly. Better make that chips and a chocolate muffin.

Once Gabrielle had polished off the snacks, she gave a great sigh and pinned Eve with a look. "So. You want to tell me about it?"

"If you're up to it. Sure." Eve pulled her chair closer. "Evidently Sam was actually..."

"Not that. There will be a time to hear about him. A better time." Gabrielle put her hand to her forehead and closed her eyes briefly. She frowned then, forming a wrinkle between her brows, but shrugged and looked back to Eve. "I was talking about you and Trey. What happened?"

Eve ran a hand through her hair. "Why do you think anything's happened?"

"Because he's not here," Gabrielle said. "And I can see you're still beaten down about something. Considering the multiple things that have been cleared up in the past...Wait. How long have I been here?"

"About twenty-six hours." Eve was afraid Gabrielle was still disoriented.

"Okay. Then in the last twenty-six hours, you've had two killers removed from your life, you celebrated your first Halloween and dropped those chains for good, plus...I'm awake and returning to my typical vibrant self." Gabrielle grinned. "So what's the hang-up?"

Eve had been wrong before. The old Gab was roaring back

to life, and a measly concussion didn't stand a chance. "It's complicated," she said, slumping back into her chair. "Suffice it to say, Trey is not who I thought he was."

"Armor's a little tarnished, huh? But aren't we all messy around the edges if you think about it?" Gabrielle lifted a meaningful brow.

If anyone was allowed to call Eve out about her issues and baggage, it was Gab. "It's more than that. He was just making sure I didn't leave Pine Creek. Can you believe that? And get this...because *Nan* asked him to. My own grandmother set me up." Eve was feeling the ire again.

"Your grandmother pulled your blonde ass out of a nothing life and dropped everything you could ever want in your lap. What was she supposed to do? Take my house, oh, and by the way, there's a nice boy I think you should meet?" Gabrielle's cheeks flushed. "Even if you and Trey didn't hit it off, she knew you would be looked after. She did it all for you even if her methods were..."

"Convoluted, controlling, and, let's not forget...post-mortem."

"I was going to say unconventional, but it all shakes out the same way. You and Trey fell for each other, and considering the circumstances, I think you could give him a little latitude." Gabrielle fell back into her pillow after she'd said her piece.

Eve felt horrible. "I'm sorry. I shouldn't be bothering you with this. You need to get back on your feet, then we'll talk."

"You can't wait for me to get out of here, Eve." Gabrielle's face was more serious than Eve had seen her in a long time. Her gypsy eyes burned with clarity and willfulness. "You have to go to him now. Before he leaves."

Eve shook her head. "He's not going anywhere. He has the business here, and his lease doesn't run out for a few months." She looked at Gabrielle's trembling fingers. "Maybe I should call the nurse."

"Don't." Gabrielle's hand shot out and snatched the call light from Eve. "You have to go to him. Tonight. You know he likes to move in the dark." She fastened her gaze on Eve. "Listen to me. Go. Now."

A chill fluttered up Eve's spine and spilled into her chest. "How do you know this, Gab?"

Her friend put her finger to her temple as she continued to stare at Eve. "I'm not sure."

~~~

He would have never considered himself a coward, but as he looked around at the newly-packed boxes littering his office, Trey had to rethink his position. He shouldn't be leaving earlier than planned, and definitely not because of a woman, but then, he had never encountered the likes of Eve Taylor. In a month's time she taken his regulated and safely plotted life and shot the hell out of it. She'd become his sole priority and focus, the only thing he really wanted or needed, much to his surprise. She'd all but wrapped him around her finger, and he'd loved every minute of it.

Now she was done with him.

The real kick in the head was that it was all his own doing. He'd seen the pitfall from a distance and had done nothing to avoid it. If he'd only come clean with Eve when he first got involved with her, maybe she would have forgiven him. But when was that exactly? Had he become a real part of her life the night they made love, or the day he'd first seen her break down and had wanted to suck the pain right out of her? Or had she had him from the start, in those snug, faded blue jeans?

It didn't matter now. All he knew was he'd spent his entire adult life avoiding commitment to any single female, and now the one he wanted to shackle himself to was giving him a pass. And he was running like a scared kid, because he knew he couldn't be this close to her every day and not be able to reach out.

He wanted those Sunday mornings with waffles or her legs

stretched across his while they watched their favorite cop show. He wanted to hear her singing off-key while she cooked her next masterpiece and for them to take Max to obedience school together, because that was one puppy who had it written all over him.

Dammit. He wanted it all.

With a curse Trey went to the next box and sealed it with packing tape. He'd always enjoyed gearing up and planning for a move. Now he felt like lead was slugging through his veins and slowing down his movements. His head hurt, and his stomach was hollow. It wasn't love he'd needed to avoid, it was the aftershock.

The thrill of moving on to new places, new faces, and new adventures had always energized Trey. There was never anything as intriguing as change, plain and simple. Until now.

He didn't have the usual motivation pumping through him at the thought of leaving Pine Creek. Of leaving Eve. Instead of heading toward something exciting, he'd be leaving something behind instead. He'd be losing the best thing that ever happened to him.

His body stilled when the doorbell rang. It could be anyone, a salesperson or someone lost, but the hope that it was Eve turned those chimes into an especially sweet sound. *Alright, Rainwater. Now you're getting downright sappy.*

But he rushed to the door anyway.

Stopping short, Trey took a steadying breath and opened up. Eve stood there...with a basket? He had no idea what to make of that. "Hey," he uttered, at a loss for anything more.

"Hey."

Eve was equally verbose, and Trey hoped that was a good sign. Shifting from one foot to the other, he asked, "Is that a going away gift? Because if it is..."

"I want to talk to you," Eve said before pressing her lips together and pushing past him as if she owned the place.

Trey didn't mind at all. "I guess I should have called, but I didn't think you'd want to talk to me." He watched as she set the basket on his kitchen counter then leaned against it, hands gripping the granite for support. "I did check on Gabrielle, though. Good to know she's going to be all right."

Trey didn't usually have to carry a conversation with Eve, and her silence was unsettling. He waited, unsure how to proceed. Then it came to him, and he felt his face heat. Why was he making this so hard? He'd never backed down from anything. And this was something he should have done a long time ago. "I'm sorry," he said, the words like sandpaper on his throat.

Eve let her lids float to half-mast and made a sound like a hiccough. Or crying. God, Trey didn't want her to cry.

"I believe you," she said, standing up straighter and turning to him. "If I know anything about you, it's that you're an honorable man. A dependable person." She pointed her finger at him. "And it's that very reliability that made me realize you were only being a friend to my grandmother. It's why I'm here tonight. I couldn't think of a selfish reason for you to have done all you did for me. You helped me when most wouldn't have, and I can't convince myself, no matter how hard I try, that it was all just to get me into bed."

"Of course not," Trey exploded. "I would never..."

"I know. I do." She held up a hand then shrugged out of her coat to lay it across a chair. "So that leaves me with a question. Why did you stay with me day and night and let something grow between us? You always said you would leave." She gestured toward the boxes. "And now you are."

Trey felt his palms break out in a sweat. How his Marine buddies would laugh to see him so nervous because' he had to face down a gorgeous blonde woman. His Viking princess. "I should have told you," he said. "I don't know when, but definitely sooner. There never seemed to be a good time. You had so much chaos in your life, and I felt partially responsible for your decision to stay here. Then it became apparent you needed someone, not just to see that you stayed in town, but to make sure you weren't hurt."

Eve listened, but her face was blank.

"I didn't feel responsible for you, Eve. I found myself..."

"What?" she asked.

"I wanted to take care of you. I couldn't stand to see you in pain, from your past or present, and I was damned if anything else was going to hurt you." Trey came closer and reached out to stroke his finger along her cheek. "I care too much to let that happen."

Eve's eyes fluttered closed, so Trey moved to embrace her.

She stepped out of his arms and walked away. "I haven't had my say yet."

~~~

"I still don't know what you're thinking. We talked about trying to make a go of this once the killer was caught, but now what foundation we had has been shaken." Eve flipped on the kitchen lights so she could see better then opened one side of her over-large picnic basket. "But what you feel doesn't matter."

Trey stood where she'd left him. "It doesn't?" He didn't look pleased.

"Well, it does, sure, but I needed to come here and tell you what's in my head, regardless." She set a box of chocolate cookies on the counter. "I've spent most of my life being afraid, Trey. Jumping at something as simple as the sound of a child's laughter, because it always took me back. I've been scared to share myself with the men I've dated, worried about their reaction if I flaked out in front of them." She gave him a serious stare. "People love crap like that in the movies, but in their girlfriend? Not really."

Trey sat on one of his stools and watched as she continued to pull things from the basket.

"So you messed up. I think that's all it was, and I was furious with you for lying." She offered him a small smile. "But I wasn't going to let anger or fear keep me from telling you I love you. Even if you choose to walk out that door anyway."

Trey's features moved ever so slightly, and she couldn't tell if he was confused, happy, or wondering why she'd brought food.

He lifted his deep brown eyes to hers and raised one finger. "Could you tell me that again?"

"All of it? Weren't you paying any attent.."

"Not all of it." He stood and walked to her, wrapping his arms around her waist so she couldn't get away. "Just the important part."

"It was all important." She huffed.

"Eve." There was warning in his tone.

With the burgeoning warmth of hope in her heart, Eve risked an impish grin. "First tell me why you've always avoided relationships. There has to be a reason."

"My father warned me," he stated simply.

Eve coughed and opened her eyes wide. "Your father warned against love? I thought you said your parents were crazy for each other."

"Oh, they are, and have been for over thirty years. My dad would look at my mom and say, 'Better be careful, Trey. Once you find the right woman, nothing else matters.'"

"Surely he didn't mean it."

"Of course he did, just not in a negative way." Trey pulled her closer. "He was deliriously in love, but to an eighteen-year-old boy with the world and all it had to offer in his sights, the sound of chapel bells equated to a death knell. I was happy for my parents but determined to avoid that fate at all costs."

"And you did. You have," Eve said, the hope she'd had deflating just a bit.

"And I was a fool." He lowered his head for a brief taste of her lips.

Eve melted into him as her body remembered its aching

need for this particular man. She was such a goner. When his mouth left hers, she asked, "But not anymore?"

"Never again. I love you, Eve." He smiled when a gasp rushed from her lungs. "I figure I've done enough avoiding. That I'd better say it, or you never would." He captured her back with his strong hands, holding her as if he'd never let her go.

Then he did. "So, what did you bring me?" He tossed his head toward the food.

Eve clapped her hands to his massive upper arms. "I had to have a back-up plan. If telling you I loved you wasn't enough, I thought I'd try the old through-the-stomach routine. Oysters, banana pudding, chocolate, wine, truffles." She bit her bottom lip. "I even got asparagus."

"Right." Trey furrowed his brow when she mentioned the last.

"Don't you remember? It's all love food." Her throat grew tight and her eyes suddenly watered, but she forged ahead. "Because I'm in love with you, and I want you to stay here. With me in my house. I don't want you to head off looking for the next great thing."

Trey cupped her face. "There is nothing better." He kissed her forehead. "And I can only move in with you on one very important condition." He nodded sagely. "Only if I can bring my dog."

A world of light swept through Eve. She whooped and jumped into his arms, then let her head fall back with a laugh. "I love you, Trey Rainwater."

His answer was his mouth on hers as he carried her down the hallway and into his bedroom. Just as he guided her feet gently to the floor, he whispered his love in her ear. It was something Eve would have to get used to, but it felt so good, she knew it wouldn't be a hardship. He loved her, and he was going to stay.

Eve let him wrap her in his arms and cover her skin with his sweet kisses. She and Trey had both learned to trust in themselves, and only because they'd found each other. He was going to make a life with her, and she was going to show him every day how much that meant.

He was her lover, her friend, and her future. Wherever they went together, whatever they did, she only had to be by his side. Her mind, her body, and most importantly, her heart... would always be safe.

If you enjoyed this book, we would love to read your review on your favorite retail or review site.

Thank you!

Suza Kates writes both paranormal romance and romantic suspense. She lives in Savannah, Georgia with her family and five ridiculously spoiled cats.

For more on Suza and her books visit

www.suzakates.com